CAPE COD NOIR

CAPE COD NOIR

CAPE COD NOIR

EDITED BY DAVID L. ULIN

AKASHIC
BOOKS

This collection is comprised of works of fiction. All names, characters, places, and incidents are the product of the authors' imaginations. Any resemblance to real events or persons, living or dead, is entirely coincidental.

Published by Akashic Books
©2011 Akashic Books

Series concept by Tim McLoughlin and Johnny Temple
Cape Cod map by Aaron Petrovich

ISBN-13: 978-1-936070-97-8
Library of Congress Control Number: 2010939098
All rights reserved
First printing

Akashic Books
PO Box 1456
New York, NY 10009
info@akashicbooks.com
www.akashicbooks.com

ALSO IN THE AKASHIC NOIR SERIES:

FORTHCOMING:

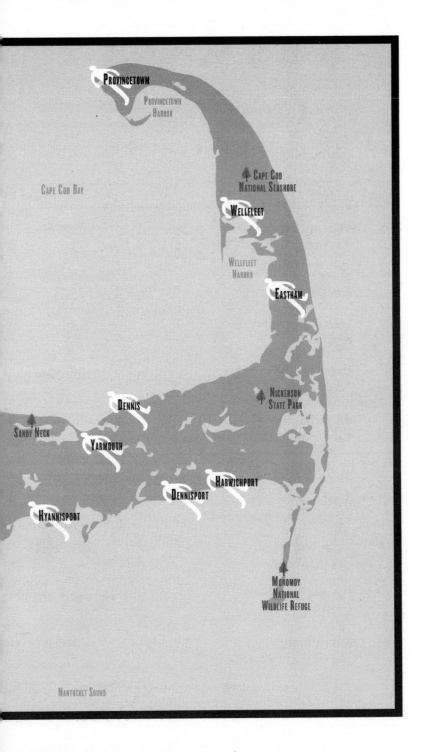

TABLE OF CONTENTS

PART III: END OF THE LINE

INTRODUCTION

I first began to think of Cape Cod in noir-ish terms during the fall of 1979. I say that, of course, entirely in hindsight, since noir was not then part of my lexicon. I was eighteen, just out of high school, on a year off that would later take me to South Texas and San Francisco. My best friend and I were making this journey together, and before we left, I spent a week at his parents' cottage in Wellfleet, where he was living alone, working as a cranberry picker, stockpiling money for the trip. Every day, he would go to work, and I would pretend to write a novel, staring out the windows at the gray October sky. At night, we would go to bars. The house was on a marshy point of land known as Lieutenant's Island, which was only an island at high tide. Some nights, we'd come back to find the road flooded, as if it had never been at all. I was not new to the Cape—I'd spent summers there, or parts of summers, since 1971—but this was a more conditional experience, more elemental and more charged. The same was true of the bars we frequented: dark places, their air thick with cigarette smoke and a kind of survivor's tenacity. Cape Cod in the off-season was a hunkered-down place, if not in hibernation exactly then in a strange, suspended state. In those days, before the Internet, when even cable TV was still scarce, there was nothing to do but drink.

Here, we see the inverse of the Cape Cod stereotype, with its sailboats and its presidents. Here, we see the flip side of the Kennedys, of all those preppies in docksiders eating steamers, of the whale watchers and bicycles and kites. Here, we see the Cape beneath the surface, the Cape after the summer people have gone home. It doesn't make the other Cape any less real, but it does suggest a symbiosis, in which our sense of the place can't help but become more complicated, less about vacation living than something more nuanced and profound.

This, it might be said, is also the case with noir, which is the dime-store genre that exposes our hearts of darkness, the literary equivalent of the blues. In noir, bad things happen to good people—or more accurately, possibilities narrow, until every option is compromised and no one ever wins. How one deals with that might seem a narrative question, but noir is less about the particulars of story than it is about point-of-view. As for the way such a point-of-view asserts itself, I think of it as stoic, stripped clean of illusion, like the faces I used to see in those off-season bars. In noir, we know that help is not coming, that the universe devolves to entropy, that everything goes from bad to worse. And yet, if this leaves us resigned or even hopeless, we have no choice but to deal with it as best we can. "I needed a drink, I needed a lot of life insurance, I needed a vacation, I needed a home in the country. What I had was a coat, a hat and a gun," Philip Marlowe observes in Raymond Chandler's *Farewell, My Lovely*, a novel that helped define the noir aesthetic, and seventy-one years later, that air of desolate clarity, of a character staring into the abyss as the abyss stares back, is still the form's defining sensibility, a cry in the darkness of a world that is, at best, apathetic, and at worst, in violent disarray.

Cape Cod Noir is an attempt to pay tribute to that perspective even as it moves beyond the traditional landscape of noir. The idea is to stretch a little, to gather writing rich in local color, while remaining true to the ethos of the genre. Here, you'll find a range of work, from the contemporary noir of Paul

Tremblay and Dave Zeltserman to the more fanciful creations of Adam Mansbach and Jedediah Berry, whose stories go in unexpected directions, asking us to question our assumptions about the form. Dana Cameron's "Ardent" takes us back to the eighteenth century, while Elyssa East and William Hastings portray a Cape Cod the tourist brochures don't recognize, marked by hard luck, history, and loss. In some stories, noir operates mostly in the background, like a whisper in the air. But this, too, is as it should be, for if there is a principle at work, it is that noir has become, in its three-quarters of a century of evolution, both stylized and supple, less a way of writing than a way of seeing, less about crime or plot or killing (although there is plenty of that in these pages) than about how we live.

What I'm saying, I suppose, is that noir forces us to face things, that it cuts to the chase. It functions, to borrow a phrase from William S. Burroughs, as a kind of "NAKED Lunch—a frozen moment when everyone sees what is on the end of every fork." We expect this when it comes to cities, where noir grew up during the Depression, or in the rural corners staked out by authors from Edward Anderson in the 1930s to Daniel Woodrell in the present day. Still, what my experiences on the Cape suggest is that noir is everywhere. You can see it in the desperate excitations of the summer people, the desire to make their vacations count. You can see it in the tension of the year-rounders, who rely on the seasonal trade for survival, even as they must tolerate having their communities overrun. You can see it in the history of the place; the Pilgrims landed first at Provincetown, after all. And after Labor Day, once the tourists have gone home, it is still a lot like it has always been: desolate, empty in the thin gray light, with little to do in the slow winter months. You drink, you brood, you wait for summer, when the cycle starts all over again.

When I was a kid, and first exploring my little corner of

the Cape, I used to spend a lot of time alone. I would ride my bike or walk for hours, watching all the summertime activities, keeping myself a bit apart. Even then, I had the sense that there was more going on than I was seeing on the surface, that there were promises that had been left unkept. This, I've come to realize, is true everywhere, but it has a different feeling in a summer place. For me, Cape Cod is a repository of memory: forty summers in the same house will do that to you. But it is also a landscape of hidden tensions, which rise up when we least anticipate. In part, this has to do with social aspiration, which is one of the things that brought my family, like many others, to the Cape. In part, it has to do with social division, which has been a factor since at least the end of the nineteenth century, when the summer trade began. There are lines here, lines that get crossed and lines that never get crossed, the kinds of lines that form the web of noir. Call it what you want—summer and smoke is how I think of it—but that's the Cape Cod at the center of this book.

David L. Ulin
March 2011

PART I

OUT OF SEASON

TEN-YEAR PLAN

BY WILLIAM HASTINGS

Falmouth

There was a time, just after I was jailed, when all I did was work, deal with my p.o., and keep my nose clean. No more shit, nothing. Just work, cash that paycheck every two weeks, stuff the bills into a hollowed-out book beneath my bed, and count the days. What I was counting for I didn't know, but looking back on it, I guess I was counting days for some type of clearing, like that moment just after a thunderstorm when the clouds part and a little light sneaks through. Except that when things finally did part and clear, I didn't get much light, but I saw it all damned well. Nice and clear, the only way you can from inside it.

To see the inside, I had to go back into a kitchen. It was a gig my p.o. lined up. He was tight with a restaurant owner. A tiny man, with child's hands and a wide forehead, he smiled when he gave me that bit of news. The job took me back home, right back to the Cape. All I had to do was learn a new system and try to keep everyone happy.

That first day I drove my old truck down Main Street, Falmouth, looking at what seven years had done to the place. A new library spread across the town green, its marble still white. The tight, weed-free circles of mulch around the trees looked fresh. The storefront windows shone, clean and filled with goods that seemed to smile at you. There were some new stores, mostly small boutiques that sold blue jeans costing more than I would take home in a single paycheck. I hung a left off Main, swung into the parking lot behind the strip of stores that housed DePuzzo's Restaurant, and pulled up next to a dumpster. I watched a guy push a shopping cart full of used car parts through the lot.

The kitchen was what I expected. It was Brazilians in the back, and they spent the whole day speaking Portuguese to each other and telling me what to do by pointing or demonstrating. They watched me and I watched them. That's all I was there to do: get the job done. I had to. The four Brazilians back there with me had been at this together for close to eight years and they had it down fast. That's how it was: two Brazilians on the line, a sauce/sauté guy and a grill/oven guy. Then there was me and another Brazilian as prep cooks. During service we did salads and desserts. An older Brazilian woman worked the dishwasher, slinging those greasy pots and pans and plates, working the steam and spray gun just trying to stay ahead. I didn't see the owner until evening.

He came in while we were winding down our prep and walked right up to me. He didn't say hello or shake my hand. He looked at me and went to the space between the walk-in and the bakery racks where the large cutting boards were kept. He picked one out, laid it in front of me, and got a yellow onion. He slapped it down onto the board.

"You know how to dice an onion?" he said.

"Yeah," I answered and reached for my knife.

"No you don't," he said. "You don't know shit about cutting an onion."

He took the knife out of my hand, split the onion in half from the root end, peeled the skin back, and did a large rough dice, fast, looking at me the whole time.

"That's how to dice an onion for the pomodoro sauce," he said. He put the knife down and walked to the front of the house.

I should have known better. It was his restaurant, his kitchen, his recipes, his system. I had to learn that, down to the finest detail. Even having done it before, I had forgotten to let it all go. Guess first impressions are best made through silence sometimes.

The owner came back in, watched me work, then asked me to step outside.

We went out the back door, into the parking lot where the summertime heat was cooking the dumpsters. There were so many flies I could hear them. I could also hear heavy traffic on the other side of the building running down Main Street. Cars driving slowly, checking out the walkers and the clean window displays. I swatted at a fly.

"You get paid every two weeks with a paycheck. I won't take uniform expenses off the top, but you don't tell them that." He jerked his head back toward the kitchen door where the Brazilians were chopping and banging pots. "You call me Mr. DePuzzo," he said. "I'll call you whatever the fuck I please."

He turned and left me standing there, the Cape air just starting to cool with the onshore breeze. A gull picked at an old french fry next to a gutter. A woman came around the corner into the lot and parked in one of the spaces for the jewelry store. She was in a Mercedes with Connecticut plates. She stretched her tanned and sandaled legs and brought herself up into the fading sunlight. She looked at me in my apron and white T-shirt, turned, and walked quickly to the rear entrance of the store.

The Brazilians were working fast to leave some sit-down time before dinner service began. Like all cooks, they wanted that time outside before the shit started. I went back to my cutting board and began prepping the garnish parsley. The other prep cook was working behind me. Something slid up between my butt cheeks and I jumped. The Brazilians all laughed. I wheeled fast and clenched my fist and the other prep cook raised a thumb in an *all's good* sign.

"You don't know how to cut a fucking *uneeon*," he mocked in English and laughed.

"I tell you something," one of the line cooks said. "You no say shit to DePuzzo, you follow us, you be okay."

"So you motherfuckers speak English?"

"Yeah, *buceta*, but the owner don't know that," the line cook said. He was wrapping blue electrical tape around the handle of a set of tongs, marking his pair. He came out from behind the line and stuck out his hand. "Gleason. That's Rener on grill and Marcello with you." We all shook hands.

"*Vai toe man o cu*," I said in Portuguese. Fuck you. Like I said, I'd been on the line before.

These guys worked clean. They didn't do lines to keep going or show up high. They'd take their shift drink out back when we were done for the night, but that was it. Hell, I was the only one who smoked butts back there. They just worked and called the waitstaff *buceta* to their faces. It was their only recourse.

The Cape Cod summers did that to them. Falmouth's population was exploding, the stress and long hours boiling with it. Going through work shirts like they were disposable because they got filthy so fast. Jamaican community expanding for the season. The Cape Verdeans battling with the Jamaicans for jobs and with knives at house parties. Eastern Europeans in on work visas cranking out eighty-hour weeks. I once worked with two Bulgarians mowing on a golf course who did five a.m. to three p.m. at the course and then went to Stop & Shop from four until two a.m. to stock shelves. Every day for four months. Then they went home to Bulgaria and bought apartments, cars, and set up a computer business. That's all they wanted, a little place of their own in the same building as their parents and enough to get them out of the cracks.

But the Brazilians. The Brazilians had originally come to the Cape because of the language. The Portuguese were already here. Now, the Brazilians worked like dogs, kept their heads down and saved, figuring they could work hard and long enough for ten years to move back home and retire.

"Man, in Brazil," Marcello told me one day, "I had a bike and a girl and the beaches, man. Your beaches here don't know. In Brazil there are guys who come up to you and sell you beer out of a cooler and the girls are walking. Man, here people just lay around and you can't drink or dance. Here I just work and there are no girls, man."

"Yeah, but you're making money."

"Money, yeah, man. But there are no girls. What do I say to American girl, man? I know English only for kitchen. What do I say when I want to go out with them? *You want special salad?* Man, you have it easy, you speak English."

"Your English is fine."

"Marcello's right," Gleason said. "You have it easy."

"What are you talking about? You run the line. You make more money than me."

Gleason just laughed and went back to making *demi glace*.

DePuzzo used to run the line, but then he got Gleason. Gleason was fresh to the Cape, called up by his brother who thought he could get him a job at the fish market where he worked. He showed up to the Cape, but it turned out there wasn't any work at the market for him. Gleason beat doors for two weeks before DePuzzo took him on as a dishwasher. All the time he was spraying dishes and racking them, DePuzzo taught him the details of prep cooking. How to move fast, how to set up the line for the service so that they didn't start calling for more ingredients until the end of the night. DePuzzo worked Gleason up a little at a time, knowing that he needed the money and wasn't dealing drugs out of the back of the kitchen or snorting up his paycheck like the last two cooks. There's a lot of coke on the Cape, bad during the summer, even worse during the winter. It's cold and there's no one. You lose a lot of line cooks that way. You lose a lot of college girls that way. I got lost that way.

Gleason worked his way up, and about the time he made prep cook, Rener and Marcello came aboard. They all knew each other back in Brazil. DePuzzo showed them the ropes, let Gleason teach them some, and kept his kitchen tight. He skimmed off their paychecks but they were working on other people's Social Security numbers so they didn't say anything. That's how they do it. They come in on a visa and when the visa runs out and an employer asks for a Social Security number to keep INS and the IRS happy, they get one from another Brazilian who's been in the country for a while.

Marcello kept on about that bike and that girl. But damn if he didn't work refinishing furniture all day and then come into the kitchen, two hours before dinner service. He had the ten-year itch too.

"What about you, G?" I asked Gleason one afternoon. "You saving up to go back to Brazil?"

He didn't answer. He just pulled his cell phone out of his pocket, flipped it open, looked at the screen, and quickly shut it. He turned away from me.

"Hey *buceta*," Rener said. "You working like us. You saving to go back to Brazil?"

"Yeah boy," I said. "You and me. We're gonna dance in the fucking streets when I get enough up. Car-knee-val!"

I bent at the waist, put my face halfway to the ground, and stretched my arms to my side like I was a swallow in flight. I pointed the index finger on my right hand toward the wall and stiffened my whole body. I shook the hell out of my leg and jabbed that finger like I was trying to poke through the air.

"This is my car-knee-val dance, boys. This is how I'm gonna do it when we go back to Brazil."

They laughed.

"You crazy, man," Rener said. "You get no girls you dance like that in Brazil."

Gleason just shook his head.

By then, I could joke with them like that. Fifteen hours a day in a summer kitchen, no one to talk to but the guys working next to you, all of you dependent on each other, and you get close, tight, real quick. Some don't, of course—they take ego in and rub everybody wrong. Those people never last, or they end up in serious shit with the other cooks. I once saw two Jamaicans take a white kid fresh out of Johnson & Wales into a restaurant basement, bend him over a flour sack, and paddle the shit out of him with a baker's peel. They had been in that kitchen five years and this boy comes fresh out of cooking school, gets put on as prep cook, and starts talking shit about the "untrained Jamaicans," slowing them down on purpose. Two days of that in the summer rush, and he got that baker's peel so bad he wouldn't sit for a week. Some nights while I was doing my bid, I'd hear crying on the tier and I'd swear it was that same college boy crying from the basement between the thwacks of a baker's peel, like a wet hand slapping a stomach.

But after I got out, I was just another motherfucker humping his shit for a p.o. and trying not to get violated right back. To hell with ego. You can't get those seven years back. So I just rolled into DePuzzo's and tried to laugh and keep those Brazilians laughing. In the heat and with DePuzzo, it was all we had.

DePuzzo came up on the Cape. I remember having some

kids with that last name in some of my high school classes. On the Cape, everybody knows everybody. Or is related to them. He spent his summers working in the kitchens on Main Street, saving money for fifteen years until he could set up a place of his own. From day one, it's been busy. Small joint, damned good food. And he takes care of the locals. Sends them a shot of homemade whiskey after their meal. Doesn't even answer when the tourists or summer residents ask what it is. Summer residents aren't local no matter how long they've lived here. You don't shovel snow in the winter or deal with the ice storms, you aren't local. Simple.

Way I began to see it in those first weeks in the kitchen, DePuzzo, at some point, had been a good guy. Stand-up. The kind you'd buy a two-buck beer for at the Elks on Wednesday and then ask after his kids. But then, after he got Gleason and those guys, he figured on something else and let it go.

I saw how far he'd come when he was set to pay my second paycheck. I'd never seen the first. He said some of it went back to him for training and the rest went to my p.o. for a finder's fee. Guess I knew then how I got that job so damn quick. And what was I gonna say? He'd just pick up the phone, call my p.o., and they'd make some shit up and violate me right back. When you're leaving prison, some guys will yell at you from the tiers, "Stay free." I intended to do just that.

Second paycheck, I figured he was gonna skim me again. Instead, he put an envelope in my hand and walked out to the front of the house. I heard him calling for the two bus-girls. Eastern Europeans. They didn't speak to me too much. Sometimes that's how it goes, front of the house keeps to their own unless they need something special or there's a complaint. Anyway, I opened the envelope and it was all there. I still heard him calling for those two girls. I stuffed the envelope into my pocket and got back to work. I made a ricotta spread, then I remembered I had to go across the lot to a small garage where we have extra refrigerators for storage. I needed lemons. I headed out the back door and across the lot. When I opened the side door to the garage, there was DePuzzo, his back to me, ass to the wind, arms behind his back holding another envelope while one of the Eastern Europeans sucked him off. When he heard me open the door, he held her head with one hand, looked over his shoulder at me, and winked. Then he flicked his wrist so I could see the girl's paycheck in his hand. It was pretty clear, the whole thing.

Back in the kitchen, side by side with Marcello cutting mushrooms, I told him about it.

"Every time," he said, "or he doesn't pay."

The next day, he came in to pay the kitchen guys. He waited the extra day because he gives them cash and doesn't want to take too much out of the bank at once.

He came in wearing jeans and a white Oxford open to his solar plexus. A thin gold chain snaked through his black chest hair. He had four stacks of bills rubber-banded in his hands. That next-day smell of booze came out of his skin in the kitchen heat. Ray-Bans on, he stood at the edge of the line next to the standing oven, slapping the stacks of bills against his palm.

The Brazilians knew exactly what to do. They all got in line in front of him, the dishwasher first. I watched from the corner, mashing potatoes. The dishwasher stepped forward and DePuzzo dropped her stack of bills on the floor. Without looking him in the eye, she bent and picked them up, and walked back to her stack of dishes. Rener stepped forward in her place and looked DePuzzo right in the eye. Guess being twenty-eight still meant something. DePuzzo twisted a sick smile and slapped the last three stacks against his open palm.

"*Buceta*," he said, and dropped the stack on the floor. Rener flinched, looked down, then bent and picked it up.

Marcello bent and got his.

Gleason was last in line, and I could see the base of his neck getting red. His jaw muscles corded as he ground his teeth. His head was tilted, his eyes shaded by his greasy kitchen-use Red Sox cap. He opened his cell phone, peered at the screen, closed it, and stepped up. He didn't look DePuzzo in the eye, but didn't look at the floor either. He just stared at DePuzzo's throat, head raised enough so the boss could see his face, his grit, but not his eyes beneath that cap.

"Stick your hand out," DePuzzo said.

Gleason looked up.

"I said stick your hand out."

Gleason raised his right hand slowly, and opened his palm. DePuzzo held the stack above the palm like he was going to drop it right there. He waited a second. Then he tossed the stack on the rubber mats and said, "Who the fuck you kidding?" as he walked out.

Every day, the Brazilians and I listened to bootleg *favela* hip-hop at top volume, or Jota Quest, or even Brazilian *sertaneja* music. I dug it. I was learning new tunes. Every day trying to crack a joke, trying to keep the dishwasher from yelling at us. She didn't like us cursing and trying to make it light before DePuzzo showed up. They stopped saying *buceta* to the staff's faces after they saw he knew what it meant. And every two weeks the Eastern Europeans went out back and the Brazilians picked their stacks off the floor. DePuzzo always handed me my money in front of the Brazilians. He figured it would turn them on me, or at least make things tough. He should have known better, he used to work the line.

One rainy Saturday, I was opening with Gleason, trying to rip through the prep work before the lunch rush. Rain means people don't go to the beach. They go to restaurants for lunch to bitch about wasting their vacation time. I was cleaning a halibut. Gleason was staring at the screen on his phone again. He hadn't put any music on yet. He was just standing and not paying much attention.

"That the ten-year plan?"

He glanced at me, the spell broken, all of him coming back from somewhere. He shut the phone and placed it on top of the industrial shelving above the buffet-style water heaters where the soups were kept warm.

"Ten-year plan," he said. "Saving every day."

"Going back to Brazil," I said.

"Going back to Brazil, buddy."

But there was something in him that reminded me of when we reach for something just beyond the fingertips. Like the first night in a cell, trying to shake the names out of your head because they're over the wall and just thinking about them makes the time grow.

"What about you? What you saving for?" he asked.

"Same as you. Except it's not in Brazil."

"You want out of here?"

I looked at the floor and felt jail.

"Yeah, G, I do. But I've got three years before they're off my back. Anyway, who's gonna hire an ex-con?"

Gleason nodded. "What you do to go to jail? You never say to me, man."

I looked away. "I was trying to save every day a little more quickly."

He nodded.

We worked through the morning and beat the lunch rush. Marcello and Rener came in later and the four of us got through the prep hard and fast and then took a break out back. We sat in chairs beneath the awning over the back door listening to the rain. The waitresses and busgirls were busy up front folding napkins and talking. Gleason and I weren't any closer since the morning, but we weren't any farther away.

That was when I heard the car tires squeal. I—we—knew. And I think all our guts dropped.

DePuzzo came tearing into the lot in his BMW X5. His windows were closed for the rain, but Van Halen was blasting so loud I could hear David Lee Roth's voice nice and clear. He gunned it across the lot, jammed on the brakes, and slid into a little turn to pull the car up in front of us. We weren't quick enough to get inside.

He shoved his door open and lurched toward us. A blond girl with bug-eye sunglasses leaned back against the passenger seat. She turned the music down so she could hear.

"What are you lazy motherfuckers doing?" he screamed. He got right up on us and stared. We got to our feet.

"Just taking a break before service," I spoke up.

"Shut up," DePuzzo said. He was drunk. Shit-stone drunk. His nostrils were red. A little of that Great Equalizer to straighten out the head.

"But . . ." I said, not knowing where it came from.

"I said shut it, or I bounce you back up to that butt-fucking prison in Norfolk."

Prison did it. I looked down when I should have looked up. I could look up in prison to stay alive, but on the outside?

"Motherfucker," DePuzzo said to Gleason, "I leave you the kitchen to run and this is how you do it? The fuck."

Gleason started to say something, then put his hand in his pocket around his cell phone. His jaw was set, his neck red.

"I said, the fuck you think is going on here?"

The girl sat up in the passenger seat, smiling at the cokehead show.

DePuzzo was so angry we couldn't move.

"I pay you motherfuckers for what? I should can your asses now for this shit. Lazy spic motherfuckers."

Rener and Marcello stared around him, but Gleason looked right at him. He started to raise his hand, as if to pause the moment, but DePuzzo stepped closer, stopping it.

He was too fast. I didn't even see his hands move. I just heard the hard thump of bone on flesh and saw Gleason go down, blood and saliva bubbling out of his mouth. He spit and I heard the rattle of a tooth hitting the pavement.

DePuzzo moved quickly. He crouched and slugged two rights to the side of Gleason's head. The bone sound made me sick. His ring cut a gash above the temple. Gleason went sea green and puked. DePuzzo drove the tip of his loafer into Gleason's ribs. They cracked, and then he stood and looked at the three of us.

"The fuck you gonna do, jailbird? The fuck you gonna do, you motherfucking illegals? Get the fuck back to work."

Gleason puked again in the rain. He moaned. I bent to pick him up. Rener and Marcello stood frozen with fear. I heard the X5's door slam, the girl laugh, and the tires squeal.

Gleason spent the night on the line, taking hard stares from the waitresses and puking into the trash can as he worked the sauté pans.

The next day we didn't joke or laugh. No music. Just head-down work. Gleason's face still held some of that green color, and he winced each time he turned or breathed too deeply. The morning and afternoon rolled on like that, silent, like the space his tooth left behind.

Gleason worked the whole shift, on the line again. The waitresses stared, and the three of us doubled our efforts to take some of the strain off him. We got through. I washed the line down with Marcello, and we took our shift drinks out back. DePuzzo hadn't shown at all.

Gleason was sitting with Rener in the parking lot next to the storage garage on chairs they'd dragged from the restaurant. I walked over. They stopped talking and peered at me. Rener said something to Marcello in Portuguese, and he turned around before he caught up to us. Then Rener stood up, stuck his hand on my shoulder, and walked toward the kitchen. Gleason nodded at the chair Rener left behind. I sat.

I had my shift drink in silence. Gleason watched. When his hands moved, I flinched. He drew his cell phone out of his pocket and flipped it open.

The screen showed two tanned young kids with dark hair and black eyes, a boy and a girl, smiling in a posed photo, the beach all around them.

"Ten-year plan," Gleason said. "They're mine. Twins. We talk every day. They're eight."

I nodded like I understood. But I didn't have kids. I hadn't left home to work for them while they were still in the womb. I didn't know shit.

"My girl's in Brazil with them. I'm going back to Brazil and stop working. Own a car repair shop so my father has a job. Enjoy my kids."

I looked at him. There was a dark, thick scab above his temple. Half-brown scars crisscrossed his forearms. I had the same scars. Ovens. Grease burns pockmarked the backs of his hands. His rubber kitchen clogs were covered in grease and food bits. The shadows under his eyes were deeper than the Cape night. Eight years.

He closed the phone and stuck it back into his pocket. I finished my drink. His eyes changed. He looked into me.

"Can you get me a gun?" he asked.

* * *

I remember I didn't sleep. I remember rain on and off for a week. Parked at the beach, I watched the storms roll in and the breakers snap in the wind. Because of my parole, I couldn't drink a beer in the cab of my truck to help put it out of my head. Shit. Stay free. But he was asking me to go back in again. Not to jail, but to what went before it.

Gleason didn't say anything at work. Marcello and Rener acted like it was all the same toward me, and I was okay with that. DePuzzo showed here and there. Never sober. Still played his paycheck games. And when I couldn't sleep, I heard Gleason's tooth hitting the pavement in the rain.

Stay free.

Two paychecks later and still I had done nothing.

Then it came on me like I was sucked out into those breakers, the air dying.

I rolled out of bed before dawn, slipped on jeans, a T-shirt, a gray hoodie, and reached below my bed for the hollowed-out book. I took what I needed, closed the book, and stuck it back. My savings.

I got into the truck and drove off the Cape to New Bedford, listening to Jimmie Rodgers the whole way.

The pay phone was still outside Taqueria la Raza on Acushnet. Probably still had that girl's number etched into the plastic handle. I went around back and knocked on the kitchen door. Balthazar opened it, sleep long out of his eyes. His old half-toothless grin lit up when he saw me. The Mexican flag tattooed on his forearm was still the same dull blue. We went into the kitchen and he made two stacks out of cases of beer for us to sit on. We sat and stared at each other and he reached out and slapped my shoulder. I told him in Spanish what I needed and he nodded.

After some *huevos rancheros*, I left the taqueria and made the call at the pay phone. Then I drove down Acushnet toward Whitman, past old houses split into two apartments. Past their chain-link fences, dying grass, and silent doors. All of it looking back at me.

Two hours later, my wallet empty, I headed back to the Cape, listening to the wind the whole way.

I kept the .45 Smith & Wesson in an oiled rag in my truck. Just couldn't bring myself to give it to Gleason right away. He was still breathing hard because of the ribs, but the green color had left his face. The scab was close to a scar. I worked and watched and tried to laugh with them, but the gun weighed on me. Everything left me but that.

Gleason kept his head down. Instead of working hard to save some time before service at night, he began going out to the storage garage during prep time to make phone calls. He knew DePuzzo didn't come around during the day, and he wanted to stay busy right through the afternoon into the night. He didn't speak much to Marcello or Rener. Nothing was broken, it was just that those fists had taken something out of the air between them. That, or forged it solid.

Payday came and DePuzzo showed with my p.o. DePuzzo was in his finest jeans and a black Harley Davidson T-shirt. My p.o. looked like his khakis and Oxford shirt would swallow him. His thin arms constantly moved, like bisected worms fighting for life. They laughed while DePuzzo gave me shit. My p.o. gave the Brazilians shit, poking them in the back and telling them to work harder. He went up to Gleason and leaned in close to the side of his face and whistled approval at the scab. DePuzzo laughed. Then my p.o. watched the paycheck routine. I waited, then went out back and watched the two of them get blowjobs from the busgirls with their hands behind their backs, each holding a paycheck.

Dusk fell. The service began and time slid into speed, into

work, into the heat and oil stink of a kitchen running at full bore. I stopped thinking, stopped feeling that weight, and kept my mind on salads, desserts, and calls for more lobsters from the line. The orders began to slow. Marcello and I stopped plating salads and desserts, and started repacking food into smaller containers.

A waitress came into the kitchen, a tall woman with gray-brown hair who'd been with DePuzzo from the get-go.

"There's an eclipse outside," she said.

We froze at the news. It was something natural, unlike our aprons and secrets. We followed her outside.

The moon was three-quarters hidden by a perfect shadow. Its light played out from the edges, leaving a crescent of ice blue along the rim of black. Its silence came at us clearly and quickly and we took it in. The waitress stood by the kitchen door. Rener sat on a flowerpot, and Marcello and I sat against the hood of a parked car. Gleason stood next to us. We craned our necks and tilted our faces toward the growing shadow, staring into the black. I could hear Gleason's slight wheeze. The shadow moved, not slow or fast, but it moved, you could sense it more than see it. Just as the shadow was about to take the moon, Gleason's cell phone rang. He answered without looking at who was calling. I was standing close enough to hear the voice come through the phone's speaker, thin and electric.

"Daddy, can you see the moon?"

The eclipse passed. I grabbed Gleason's wrist and whispered to him to wait. Everyone returned to work. I went to my truck and pulled the .45 from beneath the front seat. I closed the door and tucked the gun behind my back into my waistband. Gleason watched. He walked over to his car, a beat-up Pontiac Grand Prix with a green hood and silver body handed down through the Brazilian pipeline. He got in. I climbed into the passenger seat. The locks clicked, and I pulled out the gun.

"It's loaded," I said. "It's clean, meaning no one can trace it. When you're done with it, dump it in a salt pond at night."

I handed him the weapon and showed him how to work the safety. The chrome slide was definite against the night in the car. The black pistol grip disappeared in darkness. He took it from me with both hands, half-cradling it like a broken bird.

I spoke before he could. It was better that way.

"Take care of yourself, Gleason. Stay free."

He didn't smile, just stared at the gun. He looked at me and gave a short, sharp nod. I got out of the car and walked toward my own. Then I stopped and peered back in through the rear window. Gleason's hands were spread out a little from his sides. He was looking at his kids on his cell phone in his left hand. The gun weighed down his right.

I drove right out of that parking lot without looking back. Had to get a step ahead. After that, I lived in New Bedford for a few weeks. I stayed in a small apartment Balthazar owned down the street from Taqueria la Raza. It had a stove and a bookcase. He took the little rent he charged out of my paycheck. I worked the line with him in the kitchen, and he kept my name off the books.

We kept our eyes to the papers, our ears to the radio, and Balthazar's son checked the Internet at the library. We made calls from the pay phone. There was never any news. I couldn't chance a run back up to the Cape, and it was only a matter of time before my p.o knew I had stopped showing for work. If he cared at all. On the outside, I'm a threat to him because he's neck-deep in this shit too.

I couldn't stay with Balthazar long. No news came from the Cape. The night before I left Taqueria la Raza, I remembered the words that echoed down the tiers at me. They made me think of what we looked like beneath that eclipse, totally clear in the black, the guts of it all shining silver like an animal with its belly slit.

I've got my savings. And illegals aren't the only ones who can play tricks with Social Security numbers.

I'm on the run. Movement is freedom.

I hope he made it back to Brazil.

SECOND CHANCE

BY ELYSSA EAST

Buzzards Bay

Cunningham said that he had set up the reform school on Penikese Island so we could have a clean break with our pasts. We couldn't walk home from out here in the middle of nowhere Buzzards Bay. Couldn't hitch or swim here, either. Even boaters considered the currents dangerous where we were, twelve miles out from the Cape, past the islands of Nonamesset, Veckatimest, Uncatena, Naushon, the Weepeckets, Pasque, and Nashawena, just north of Cuttyhunk. There was no Cumbie Farms, no Dunkin' Donuts, no running water, Internet, or cell service here. Not even any trees. Just a house made from the hull of an old wooden ship that had run aground. Me and six other guys, all high school age, who were lucky to be here instead of in some lock-up, lived with Cunningham and the staff, most of whom were also our teachers. The school had a barn, chicken coop, woodshop, and outhouse. The only other things were the ruins of a leper colony, a couple of tombstones that Cunningham liked to call a cemetery, and the birds. Lots of birds. Seagulls, all of them, that hovered over this place like a screeching, shifting cloud that rained crap and dove at our heads all day.

This was our clean slate, a barren rock covered in seagull shit.

We had to leave most of our things behind on the mainland when we were shipped out here on a rusty lobster boat called *Second Chance*, but our pasts couldn't help but follow us here anyway. We were always looking over our shoulders and finding them there. Depending on the time of day, we were either chasing the shadows of our pasts or being chased by them. We cast them out over the water with our fishing nets. They were with us when we hoed the garden, split wood, and changed the oil to keep *Second Chance*, the school's only boat, in working order. We watched them tackle and collide and fall to the ground next to us while we played football and beat the shit out of each other much like the waves that endlessly pounded this rock. I just wondered when our pasts would pick themselves up, dust themselves off, and walk away. You could say that's what we all wanted them to do. Least that's what I wanted for mine.

I never meant to be in the car that killed that girl. It was like that was someone else, not me. Like I wasn't even there. But I was.

Mr. Riaf, my court-appointed lawyer, had said that the hardest thing out here on Penikese was figuring out how to survive the other guys. "Someone always cracks," he said. "Don't let it be you, kid."

Freddie Paterniti said that when D.Y.S. told him he could go to school on an island for a year instead of being thrown back in the can, he thought he was gonna be spending his days jet-skiing. Everybody gave Freddie a load of shit for being such a stupid fuck though they had all thought the same thing. Me, I never admitted to knowing better.

Instead of jet skis, cigarette boats, and chicks in bikinis, we got Cunningham, the school's founder, an ex-Marine who fought in Vietnam and looked like Jean-Claude Van Damme crossed with Santa Claus. Cunningham believed that our salvation lay in living like it was 1800, but the lesson wasn't about history: "You boys were chosen to ride *Second Chance* here because you have shown a demonstrated capacity for remorse for your crimes. We're here to teach you that your actions literally create the world around you. By creating everything you need with your own bare hands, you can re-form the person you are deep within. And you can take that second chance all the way back to a new place inside."

That's why we carried water, slopped pigs, caught fish, dug potatoes, gathered eggs, and built tables and chairs, and if we didn't, we wouldn't have had anywhere to sit and nothing to eat.

We chopped a lot of firewood that was brought in on *Second Chance* from Woods Hole. If we got pissed off—which was often—we were sent out to chop more. At first our muscles ached for days. The feel of the axe ricocheted up our elbows, into our shoulders, our skulls. But we got stronger. Soon we split wood and dreamed of splitting the take, splitting open girls' thighs, splitting this place, this life.

We were constantly making our world in this nowhere place, chopping it to bits, and redoing it all over again, but we couldn't remake what we had done to earn our way here.

"Boys," Tiny Bledsoe would say when we made the cutting boards that were sold in a fancy Falmouth gift shop to help fund the school, "consider yourselves to be in training for Alcatraz. Soon you'll graduate to making license plates and blue jeans!" Each time Tiny said this Freddie hit the woodshop floor, laughing.

Freddie and Tiny were an odd couple. Freddie: sixteen, short, oily, wall-eyed, with the whiniest high-pitched Southie voice you could imagine. Tiny: seventeen, a lumbering, club-footed giant who came from East Dennis. They were nothing like me and my big brother Chad, but they reminded me of us in their own way. They both claimed to have killed people. That was their thing. Their special bond. Something that Chad and me have now too.

* * *

That girl's mother sent me a picture of her, lying in her casket. It looked like one of those jewelry boxes lined in pink satin with a little ballerina that spins while the music plays. All you have to do is turn the key and that ballerina comes to life, but there's no key on a casket. Just some motor at the gravesite that lowers the box into the ground. My little sister Caroline had one of those jewelry boxes. There was nothing in it but some rings she got out of those grocery store things you put a quarter in. The rings weren't worth anything, but Chad convinced me to steal her jewelry box anyway.

Freddie and Tiny. It was never Tiny and Freddie, though Tiny was a foot taller. Even Cunningham and our teachers caught on, always saying "Freddie and Tiny" like "I got Freddie's and Tiny's homework here!" "Freddie and Tiny are going to lead us in hauling traps!" "Freddie and Tiny . . ."

One day early in the year, Ryan Peasely was rolling his eyes in mechanics class and mumbling behind Cunningham's back, "Freddie and Tiny sucked my cock. Freddie and Tiny ate my ass." It seemed like no one could hear him other than me, but Tiny had sonar for ears. He clamped down on Ryan with a headlock in no time flat. Freddie then whispered into Ryan's ear that he would kill him by running a set of battery chargers off *Second Chance*'s engine block up his ass.

Ryan is from Wellesley. Just cause he used to sell dope to his private school buddies he thinks he's better than all of us, but Ryan just about shit his pants that day. Cunningham punished Freddie and Tiny by making them clean out the outhouse, but Freddie didn't seem to care. He nearly died from laughing so hard.

When Freddie laughs he sounds like the trains that went through the woods down the road from the cul-de-sac where

I grew up back in Pocasset: "A-Huh-a-huh-a-huh-a-huh. A-Huh-a-huh-a-huh-a-huh."

It was also Chad's idea to take Caroline's jewelry box and set it on the train tracks. Bits of that doll went flying everywhere. You could still hear the music playing long after the train left.

Caroline cried so hard after she saw her jewelry box was missing, I went out and gathered up all the pieces of the ballerina that I could find. I wanted to give them to Caroline and make her feel better, but Chad shook his head and said, "What people don't know can't hurt them."

I threw the pieces of the ballerina in the yard later on. I still remember watching the bits of pink plastic and white gauze fly from my hand.

Chad came into the room we shared later that night and said, "You're a real man now, you know that, kid?"

I was only eight, and he was thirteen but he had started shaving. He knew what it meant to be grown up.

Learning how to be a man is part of Penikese's chop-wood-carry-water philosophy. Penikese isn't like being in jail, boot camp, or even regular school, though we can earn our G.E.D. and learn a couple of trades like fishing and woodworking. It's some of all of these things in an Abe-Lincoln-in-a-log-cabin kind of way. Cunningham leads us on walks and tells us stories about the island and calls it history. Wood shop is where Mr. Da Cunha teaches us how to make furniture, which is also his way to con us into measuring angles and calling it geometry. We whittle pieces of wood along with the time; we're stuck here for a year unless we fuck up, which means getting shipped off to juvie, which none of us wants though there is something about this place that makes everything bad we've ever done seem impossible to escape. Like the fact that the house where we're living is a ship going nowhere.

At night we sit by kerosene lanterns and do homework around the kitchen table or play pool, except for Bobby Pomeroy who spends a lot of time in the outhouse where we're all convinced he's busy beating wood.

Bobby grew up on a farm somewhere in Western Mass, where he was busted for assault and date-raping some girl. Cause he's a farm boy, he teaches us things that even Cunningham doesn't know. Useful things. Like how to hypnotize a chicken.

We'd only been here for a few weeks when Bobby grabbed the smallest chicken in the coop by its feet and lifted it, so it was hanging upside down. The chicken was squawking and clucking, but as soon as Bobby starting swinging it around and around it quieted down. "That'll learn ya," Bobby said, then set the chicken back on the ground. Next thing you knew that chicken was walking in circles and bumping into things, like it was drunk. We all laughed our asses off, but for Tiny and DeShawn.

"That's not fucking funny," Tiny said.

"Whassamattuh?" Freddie said.

"It's just a little chicken."

"You feckin' killed some girl and you're getting ya panties in a wad over some dumb chicken that's gonna end up in a pot pretty soon heyah?" Freddie said.

"Just make it stop," Tiny replied. His eyes were turning red, his lower lip quivering, but the chicken was still spinning around bumping into things. We couldn't stop cracking up.

"Fucking knock it off, you assholes!" Tiny yelled.

Then the chicken lay down and stopped moving altogether. The chickens in the coop went quiet too. All we could hear was the wind whistling like a boiling kettle.

"That's fucking sick," Kevin Monahan said. "You're sick, Tiny. Killing your own girlfriend and defending some stupid chicken." Kevin was in for burning down an apartment building in Springfield while cooking up meth with his father. Some old lady's cat died in the fire.

"Arson ain't no big thing compared to killing a pretty little girl, pansy," Freddie said.

Bobby snapped his fingers over the bird, which rolled onto its feet and started walking again.

"That's like some voodoo or something," DeShawn said, moving away from Bobby like he was a man possessed.

Bobby had power over that chicken just like Freddie had power over Tiny and Chad had power over me.

Chad and me used to be like Freddie and Tiny: inseparable. I followed Chad everywhere, did whatever he did, and whatever he wanted me to do. Now he's doing time on a twenty-year sentence on account of our accident. On account of me.

Sometimes we got Saturday-afternoon passes to Woods Hole on the mainland. Saturdays in "the Hole" were good until Freddie convinced Tiny to steal *Second Chance* and take it over to Osterville where they said they were going to break into some boats cause Ryan Peasely told them how much money he cleared dealing from his dad's summer house out thataway.

As we ferried over that late September day, Tiny said, "I ain't doin' it." Stubby Knowles, our mechanics and fisheries teacher who also captained *Second Chance*, was inside the wheelhouse and couldn't hear us over the sound of the engine, the wind, and the squawking gulls.

"Whassamattah? You chickenin' out?" Bobby asked.

"Fuck you," Tiny shot back.

Tiny didn't like Bobby much. After the chicken-swinging incident, Tiny asked if taking care of the chickens could be his chore and his alone, like he wanted to keep the birds safe from Bobby. No one fought him for the honor.

"Bawk!" Bobby said. Freddie snorted with laughter. They high-fived.

Tiny stared so hard at Bobby he could have burned two holes straight through him with his eyes. Bobby shrank. Tiny was twice his size and could have easily snapped him in two.

Tiny started to laugh that kind of laugh that sounds weirdly close to crying. "Fooled yas, I did," Tiny said. But Tiny hadn't fooled anyone. He was only staying in because he didn't want Bobby to take his place as Freddie's best.

As soon as we stepped off the boat, Freddie said, "Listen, homies, we gonna bust this shit up like something real," like we were a bunch of brothers who had escaped Rikers on some wooden raft and sailed our way up to the Cape to terrorize all the rich people.

"DeShawn, my nigga, you reel in da ho's for me."

Freddie always talked like a gangsta rapper to DeShawn, so did Bobby. Two boys, as white as they come. Even Freddie, though he's Italian, as pale as the moon. Tiny just stood to the side looking confused, waiting for them to get it over with and talk like their old selves again.

Bobby and Freddie worshipped DeShawn cause he's black and from Dorchester. DeShawn wouldn't say anything about why he was here, but you could always see wheels turning behind his eyes, going somewhere way the fuck far away and running us over on his way there.

Whenever DeShawn got that look on Freddie always said, "Like, DeShawn my man, you and me relate, homes, cuz your shit is real, brother, just like my shit is real, a'ight?"

Freddie never seemed to notice the look that came over

DeShawn's eyes when he talked to him. Then again, if he did notice he didn't seem to care. It's kind of like Chad saying what you don't know can't hurt you, only with Freddie it was pretending that you don't know, like pretending that De-Shawn didn't hate him would help keep him from getting his ass kicked all over the Hole.

The night of the accident, back in August, I pretended everything was okay.

"Dudes," Chad had said to some friends of his who pulled up next to us in front of the Cumbie Farms, "I bet you a thousand dollars my little brother and I can jack a car faster than you."

It had been a long time since Chad and me had broken into a car and I doubted he and his friends had any money, unless they were dealing, which they probably were, but I didn't want to know. I hadn't seen much of Chad in three years, not since he had turned eighteen and joined the Army.

"Why you wanna go fight the war?" I asked him before he left.

Chad pointed to his head and said, "Gotta be easier than fighting the war inside."

It wasn't that Chad was a bad guy, it was that he was good at things you weren't supposed to do like breaking into places and stealing shit. And Chad had this ability to not get caught, which, in a twisted way, made me and Caroline think he was going to do well being off in the Army fighting terrorists. But not even Mom could explain why Chad was eventually discharged and came back from Afghanistan with scripts for all kinds of things, except to say, "It's as if your brother has taken lots of bullets inside his heart, Tommy. You can't actually see the place that got hurt, but if you could, you'd know how badly he's suffering." Sometimes I could see it written all over his face, though, like that night sitting and drinking in the car at Cumbie's.

"Remember how good it used to be?" Chad asked. "You and me, droppin' it like it's hot?" He took a swig from his beer and wiped his mouth.

I remembered how it was, letting Chad talk me into sneaking into someone else's garage, their car, their house, riding away on their bikes with PlayStations and laptops stuffed into our backpacks. It was everything I had wanted to forget about myself, but for Chad. Once he left, I started trying to clean up my act, but now Chad was back and he had a thousand dollars riding on my back.

"Yeah, that was cool," I said as we finished off our beers before heading out to find a new ride for the night. Maybe it's cause we grew up without a dad, but it was easier to lie than to admit that I never wanted to do any of that stuff, I had just wanted to be with Chad. "Welcome home, bro," I said. "It's good to have you back."

Chad passed me another bottle of beer. As he steered the car onto the dark road, I felt myself move back to that place I had been trying to get beyond, but now that Chad was home safe I knew I had never wanted to leave.

We parked behind the valet parking booth next to the Pocasset Golf Club clubhouse. Chad took a lumpy sock out of a military duffle bag and tucked it inside his jean jacket. "BRB, dude," he said, and got out of the car and went inside the booth.

The booth sat there, dark, motionless, silent, with a blue glow coming through the blinds. I sat and downed another beer, tasting its bitterness, waiting for fifteen minutes, maybe more, for Chad to emerge.

Chad got into the car and held up a set of keys to a '66 Mustang.

"Whoa, so how did you do that?" Like I needed to ask.

"Just a little barter. This way we get the sweet ride, we gas 'er, and return 'er by eleven. Ain't no need to go breakin' no law."

Chad texted his friends: *Got the ride boyz. Where U @?*

In Woods Hole, we all gathered back at the dock at five, like always. Stubby was yelling into his cell phone, pacing back and forth. *Second Chance* was gone.

Freddie and Tiny never made it to Osterville. A coast guard patrol boat picked them up near Popponesset where the boat had run out of gas. They said they had planned to bring it back in time and would have filled it up, but they didn't have any money because of school policy so it wasn't their fault *Second Chance* ran out of gas.

The Mustang at the golf club had a full tank. So did Chad. Whatever he had done in that booth had shot his eyes through with blood.

We drove to where his friends were sliding a slim jim into the door of some shit Toyota.

"Well, I guess you won," one of his friends said and gawked at our ride.

Chad and I had a few beers left, but his friends were out so Chad thought it would be cool to race to the liquor store over on the other side of the Bourne Bridge.

"The old Bridge Over Troubled Waters, ha ha ha," his friend, the one who was driving, said.

"Whoever gets there last is buying," Chad commanded, then laid down enough rubber to leave them behind in a cloud of smoke.

The more fucked up and dangerous Chad's idea was, the more likely it was that he could pull it off. That's what set him apart. That's why I loved him and feared him all the same. Why I thought he was going to come home a hero. Why we were going to beat his friends across that bridge and they were gonna be buying us a case of Bud and a bottle of Goldschläger, suckahs.

Later on, the cops kept asking me what I said to try and stop Chad from "stealing" the Mustang or from cooking up Ritalin and Talwin—which, they explained, is as good as mixing coke and heroin—in that valet booth, or even putting back half a case of beer while driving. They made a big deal out of the drinking and driving as if everyone else around here didn't do it. But I never said anything to stop Chad. It wasn't just because I knew there was no stopping him once he set his mind to a thing, or that I knew how badly he needed to win at something since coming back home. It was that I had wanted us to win together.

Cunningham ended up revoking Saturday privileges because we all knew that Freddie and Tiny were planning to steal the boat and never said anything about it.

Bobby tried to reason with Cunningham: "But if you had never known about it you never would've gotten upset, so you don't need to punish us because there was no reason to tell you. Besides, Tiny had been talking about stealing *Second Chance* for weeks. Until they didn't come back, nothing bad had happened, so what was there to say?"

Freddie and Tiny were punished with extra wood chopping. Bobby had to shovel shit all week.

I still remember what it felt like going over the bridge in that Mustang. All I could feel was how high and fast we were, Chad and me together, set free from something inside.

"Pop me another cold one," Chad said.

I reached into the backseat, grabbed one of our beers, and cracked open the bottle as we were nearing the exit. But we were in the left-hand lane and the exit ramp was already in sight. Chad's friends were right behind us. Chad floored the Mustang to get ahead of an SUV next to us and ferry over straight onto the ramp. But the SUV driver gave us the finger and accelerated too, cutting us off from the lane. Chad slammed on the brakes. My head whipped forward. The beer went flying out of my hand. The bottle sailed into the windshield and exploded. A spray of beer stung Chad's eyes. He lifted his hands off the wheel. Shards of glass cut his face, his hands.

My shoulder hit the window. The seat belt cut into my neck. And the Mustang slammed into the driver's-side door of a Honda Civic that was trailing the SUV.

Katelyn Robichard, UMass Dartmouth freshman and Corsairs striker, 2009 Little East Conference Women's Soccer Offensive Player of the Year, was at the wheel of the Honda. Her seat belt stayed secured, but her airbag didn't inflate. And pretty little Katelyn Robichard snapped forward at her waist, just like a jack-in-the-box that sprung up out of its lid and collapsed.

Freddie and Tiny were out doing their time, chopping a forest full of wood for the third day in a row, when a periwinkle shell flew out of the clouds and pelted Freddie in the head.

"Muthahfeckah," Freddie muttered and slammed his axe down on a piece of wood.

Another shell came hurling toward him. He swung at the clouds with his axe and yelled, "Come down here, you bitches! You want a piece of me? I'll show you a piece of me, ya shit-eating birds."

The sky filled with cackles, like God was slapping his thigh at the sight of Freddie blowing his top.

A gull dive-bombed his head and tore at his hair. A shrieking Freddie covered his head with his one free hand and continued swinging his axe overhead. More gulls flew at him. Tiny started throwing pieces of wood into the sky.

We hated those giant, hungry clouds of birds, but we hated Freddie and Tiny more for getting us all in trouble.

Except for Bobby, who was in the outhouse, we were all inside supposedly doing homework and chores. But we got up to watch the big show out the kitchen window. Freddie was swinging his axe around like some murderous fuck. "I'm wicked pissa sick o' bein' out here with all these birds shitting on me all the goddamned time!"

"It's not the birds that're causing the problem," Cunningham said. He stood on the porch, the picture of calm. His voice sounded out low and deep, like a horn through the fog.

Tiny could always tell when Cunningham was about to deliver one of his living-like-a-homesteader-is-good-for-you lectures. "Astern, astern! Eye-roller coming on!" he would shout, like a rogue wave that only he could see was moving through Cunningham. But for now, Tiny was still throwing pieces of wood in the air at the gulls. Da Cunha came busting out the back door and beelined straight for Tiny, throwing him down in a hammerlock.

"It's you, Freddie," Cunningham said. "The birds are just birds. You're the one choosing to see it as an attack. Life is full of people and things, situations that are going to dump shit on you. You can't control that. You can only control your reaction to it. You have to learn your Pukwudgies."

"Feck you and your fekwudgees!" Freddie shouted. "I'm sick of getting it in the ass from you pricks." The gulls shrieked and laughed as they followed Freddie, who stormed off toward the water with that axe.

Da Cunha still had a grip on Tiny, who turned limp as he watched Freddie disappear. "It's not fair!" Tiny sobbed. "It's not fair. It wasn't my idea to steal the boat. I didn't want to take it. It's all Freddie's fault."

It was true. It had been Freddie's idea, but Bobby had tried to paint it like it was Tiny's doing. Cunningham said it didn't matter whose idea it was. They had stolen *Second Chance* together.

Da Cunha released Tiny, who rolled on the ground. Stubby appeared. He and Da Cunha went out toward the water, after Freddie.

"What's a Pukwudgie?" DeShawn asked.

"Come on," Cunningham said. "Time for a little island history lesson." Cunningham gave Tiny a hand, helping him up. He wrapped his arm around Tiny, and led the rest of us up the hill. As we rounded the graveyard we could hear Freddie's shouts of "Feck you, you feckin' narc, Tiny!" go by on the wind.

The stone ruins of the leper colony looked like the bones of a giant that had been buried there and gradually unearthed. As soon as we passed them for the windward side of the island, the seagulls that had been trailing us dropped off. The wind started to howl and whine.

Ryan and Kevin went back cause they were on the evening's cook shift. DeShawn gave me a look like he didn't want to walk back with Ryan, who was nothing but a snot-nosed pain in the ass, or Kevin, who was bound to do something stupid like walk us off a cliff. Maybe he was also scared that Freddie was still running around with that axe. No matter. I could tell by the way Cunningham had his arm around Tiny that he wasn't going to let him go anywhere. This walk was for Tiny. Maybe I knew it was also for me.

I put up my hands as we crashed into that girl's car, but I could still see her face. Her body jackknifing. Her head and chest flying over the steering wheel, toward the windshield.

They call it safety glass because when your head hits the windshield it shatters but stays in place so that it catches you, like a net. If that fails, and you're airborne, it crumbles like a cookie so you don't get cut. But chunks of metal went flying. That girl didn't stand a chance.

Sometimes I feel as if I'm made of safety glass, as if everything inside me has shattered yet somehow stays intact. But Chad was all cut up inside, like that broken beer bottle, which sliced up his face.

Everything would've been okay if I hadn't handed Chad that beer.

Cunningham took us to a crumbling stone courtyard that gave us a little protection from the wind. Me, Tiny, and DeShawn sat down on some old stone benches where we could see the water and some lights from New Bedford, on the other side of the bay. Cunningham cleared his throat, like he had been practicing some speech he'd prepared.

"After the leper colony closed, a caretaker lived out here with his wife and two sons. They were the only people on the island. Then one of the kids killed the other. They said it was a freak accident, but anyone who knew this place and that family knew the truth. It was because of the Pukwudgies.

"The Pukwudgies were these little demons, no bigger than your hand, that made the Wampanoags' lives miserable. They broke their arrows, bored holes in their canoes, and ruined their crops. It would not be inaccurate to say they were the Wampanoag equivalent to having a seagull defecate on your head, but as tiny as they were, they had great power over the Wampanoag giant Moshup and his sons." When he said "giant," Cunningham shot Tiny a meaningful look.

"One day, Moshup declared war against the Pukwudgies. He gathered his sons and set out across the Cape to hunt them down. At night, while Moshup and his boys were sleeping, the Pukwudgies snuck up on Moshup's sons, blinded them, and stabbed them to death. Moshup buried his sons along the shoreline. He was so aggrieved he covered their gravesites with rocks and soil to create enormous funerary mounds. In time the ocean rose, carrying the mounds—and the boys' remains—to here. All the islands here in Buzzards Bay—Naushon, Pasque, Nashawena, Cuttyhunk, and Penikese—are what remains of the great giant's sons."

The wind was threading its way through the holes in the stonework, curling itself around us, sliding across the backs of our necks.

"You mean we're sitting on some Indian grave?" DeShawn asked.

Cunningham nodded. DeShawn shuddered.

In the silence, you could hear the ocean churning underneath the wind. That was when I heard what sounded like a small mewling thing. I looked around. DeShawn caught my eye and nudged his head over toward Tiny who started bubbling up like a hot two-liter that had just been cracked open. "She-she-she—"

DeShawn scratched at the ground with a rock. It smelled like fresh dirt.

"I didn't mean to hurt her," Tiny gurgled. "I loved her."

Tiny was now going like a geyser. I just kept watching the water, the blackness moving out there, flashing like silver in the moonlight.

"I liked her so much."

DeShawn looked like he wanted to dig his way to China with that rock, anything to get out of there. Then he suddenly stopped, like he remembered he was digging on someone's grave. He sat on his hands and glanced away.

Tiny curled up in a ball and put his hands over his head,

as if he was scared he was gonna get hit. Cunningham scooped him up like Santa Claus picking up some big fat kid who was crying because he wanted a new fire truck, only it wasn't a truck Tiny wanted. It was a new life. That was all Tiny wanted. At age seventeen.

The world is full of people like us. Floating out here like these half-sunk islands covered in shit. We're drifting through your city, your town, cutting across your backyard, walking up your fire escape, sliding a slim jim between your car window and door, slipping into your leather bucket seats that smell like money—your money. We're wiring your ignition, busting your satellite radio, rifling through your shit, tossing out manuals and hand sanitizer, tissues, registration, and pens, until we find that emergency envelope full of freshly printed twenties. We coast along your streets, caught up in the current of something swirling inside us, riding swells of blacktop anger with the wind at our backs. We don't really want your car, your daughter, your jewelry, your things. Just like with you, that shit helps us forget why it can hurt to be alive, but only for a little while.

We snuck away, DeShawn and me, leaving Tiny to be lectured by Cunningham about "crossing the treacherous waters," "a new day dawning," and "making the journey called Second Chance." Somewhere behind us on that dark path, we could hear Tiny say he wanted to be different, but he just didn't know how. He just didn't know how, he repeated again and again, the sound of his voice echoing in the wind.

Later that night, we could hear Tiny crying himself to sleep, rocking back and forth. It was like we were all at sea, rolling through the waves of regret crashing around inside him.

"Feckin' A," Freddie said. "Feckin' knock it off, you pansy." Freddie had calmed down since earlier. At dinner that night he was so cool it was spooky, like Stubby and Da Cunha had worked him up something good.

"Shut up," DeShawn said. "I'm sick of you and your freak-ass shit."

"Yo, homes," Freddie said. "I didn't mean nuthin' by it. You and me, we're cool, a'ight?"

"No," DeShawn answered. "We ain't never been cool."

We had all been pretending to be asleep, just waiting for Tiny to knock it off, which he did, eventually. Then the house slowly quieted down as the other guys stopped tossing and turning and dozed off for real. But after all of Tiny's tears, that silence kept me awake.

I stared out the window and watched the moon rise higher like a giant eyeball staring out over the hill where the leper cemetery was. In the silence, I could tell someone else was awake and knew I was up too. And he—or it—was just waiting for that moment when I would fall asleep. I lay as still as possible and listened to the waves against our island rock. It was like we were part of some cycle of nature, meant to crash up against things forever.

Eventually, I fell asleep.

In the morning, I could hear Cunningham racing down the stairs. Tiny screaming. Voices coming in from outside. De-Shawn and me flew out of bed at the same time, put on our jeans and boots, and ran downstairs. Ryan, Kevin, and Bobby came stumbling out of bed behind us.

Opening the door, I heard it. Like so many little creatures, Pukwudgies maybe, sobbing or laughing—I couldn't tell which—in the wind. I looked around for them, but I didn't see anything. DeShawn pointed to the chicken coop.

Cunningham, Da Cunha, and Stubby just stood and stared. Tiny was on his knees, inside the coop. No one was saying a word.

The chickens, which were usually running all over the place by the morning, crowing and cock-a-doodle-dooing, were trying to stand on their little chicken legs, but as soon as they got halfway up, they fell over. Someone or something had come in the middle of the night and broken all their legs, just snapped them like twigs. The chickens kept trying to stand, flopping over, and crying out. Lying there, dying, but wanting to live.

At least twenty pairs of beady little eyes looked up at us for help, looked at us for nothing cause there was nothing we could do but put them out of their misery.

Tiny was running his fingers through the dirt, tears streaming down his face. Even Bobby looked like someone had just punched him in the gut.

Freddie was the last person to come out of the house. He strolled up to the chicken yard and didn't even try not to laugh.

Tiny picked up one of the littlest birds. I couldn't tell if it was the same chicken Bobby had hypnotized. They had all grown some in the past couple of weeks and most of them had looked the same to me anyway. But Tiny held that chicken close to him and rocked it like it was a baby he was going to do everything in his power to try and save.

Sometimes I wish I could have cried like Tiny did. After Chad and me hit that car, I didn't even realize there were tears streaming down my cheeks. There were sirens and lights. Cops and paramedics sawing through car doors with their Jaws of Life.

The last thing I remember was Chad sitting there, patting the dashboard of the Mustang and saying, "Guess we're gonna have to take this one out and shoot it."

The next day we all watched the fog swallow *Second Chance* whole. Freddie was onboard, being shipped out to "Plymouth

Rock"—*Plymouth County Correctional Facility,* as it reads on the books, where all the child murderers go.

Tiny was different after that. I guess DeShawn and me changed too. We helped Tiny dig a grave and bury all the chickens. Cunningham showed us some books in the school library where we read up on Indian funerary mounds. We gathered up some rocks and soil and covered the birds' grave the Wampanoag way.

Tiny, DeShawn, and me never talked about the chickens or how we became friends, if that's what we really were. We didn't talk about much. But we did our chores or whatever, and never said anything, which was like saying a lot because it wasn't like being with someone you can talk to but don't. It was pretty much all right.

ARDENT

BY DANA CAMERON

Eastham

Having reached a despairing state, Anna Hoyt, as a last resort, found herself in church.

Her legs betrayed her, and she sat down heavily, the roll of winter seas having taught her a different way of walking in the weeks during the passage from London. At least the salt air in the meetinghouse was mingled with fresh, without the closeness of shipboard life. The hard plank seat of the pew was welcome because it did not move, the silence of the church a blessing after the unceasing roar of wind and waves.

She was no more than hours away by sail from Boston across Massachusetts Bay, in the town of Eastham. She longed to see her tavern, the Queen's Arms, and had sacrificed much to preserve her livelihood there. Her trip to London had opened her eyes to the restrictions of rank and sex, the power of learning, and the astonishing ease with which men could be manipulated, even to murder. And while she knew in her heart she belonged in Boston, she also knew that her former life pouring beer for sailors and fishermen was impossible. She had money now, and a glimpse of the wider world that fed a kind of ambition, but for what, she did not know. The question had plagued her over the weeks of travel: if she could not be what she had been, and was not allowed to be what she might want, what would she do?

Once, she'd actually climbed the stairs from her quarters on Mr. Oliver Browne's ship *Indomitable* and gone to the railing, looking at the waves: angry, white-capped slate. She hesitated, then would not jump, for anger at those who'd placed her in this position: the men who conspired for her property, the men who would use her quick wit for themselves, the laws that constrained her as a woman.

The welcome rage sustained her.

Just before dawn on the last day, within sight of land, she observed an unholy light. Beautiful tongues of orange and pink and green stretched out into the sky, and Anna realized she was watching a building burn.

"Someone's lost money tonight," said her traveling companion, Mr. Adam Seaver. Then: "We must stop here, to attend an errand. They'll put us ashore."

No doubt it was on behalf of their mutual benefactor and employer, Mr. Browne. Still answerless, Anna was neither relieved nor angered by the delay; she merely nodded.

But the Sunday morning bustle at their inn reminded her of her own establishment. She glanced at the exquisitely dressed manikin on her table, but Dolly had no answers for her. And when she turned to her well-worn Bible for comfort and instruction, her eyes blurred so she could not read. Denied this, she pulled on her blue velvet cloak and left.

The village was set against sandy dunes on a sheltered harbor, a spit of land that curled protectively against the bay. Outside the inn, she saw a crowd standing around the burnt ruin of the building she'd seen from the ship. No more fiery beauty here: heavy timbers burned to charcoal jutted out from the collapsed wreckage against the clear sky, like so many black marks on a blotter. Turning away from the gathered townspeople, Anna saw a man in a towering fury shaking a boy half his size. The child's thin arms and legs practically rattled with the movement, and tears streamed down his filthy face.

"You little shit of a liar!" Flecks of spittle flew from the man's lips. "First you say you saw a man, then a girl. Which is it?"

"Both!"

The man dropped the boy, and kicked him until his anger was dissipated and the boy stopped moving.

Anna shook her head. She walked until she found the meetinghouse by the creek.

She did not pray. She didn't have it in her to ask for favor. The church was only another container for her emptiness. She went through the rituals absently, without solace.

But there was information to be had. The vehemence of the sermon, drawn from Leviticus, about the land turning to whoredom, alerted Anna. The red and sweating face of the preacher, and his steadfast refusal to look anywhere near the lovely lady in the third row, confirmed it. The preacher would have chosen a milder topic if he hadn't been caught doing something he shouldn't.

Two women in front of Anna barely concealed their amusement. "Come Monday," one whispered to the other, "she'll be right back at it. Where else would our betters get their release?"

They ceased only when the warden raised his eyebrows. Anna added this observation to her present perplexity. The lady who seemed to be the object of the sermon hadn't asked permission to ply her trade. She was in church, nodding with the best of them, free to ignore the implications. She was certainly doing well for herself, in one of the better pews, modestly but well dressed.

She makes her way well enough, asking no leave of anyone, Anna thought. *If it is my will I serve, what do I want?*

As the preacher delved into the exact nature of the hellfire that awaited sinners, Anna stood, ready to leave. There was nothing for her here, only more men with more words to shape the world for themselves. She had to leave or go mad.

Something stopped her, and she almost rebelled against it, but pausing showed her the reason. Out the window, she saw him peering in furtively. Blond hair, more ash-gray now, but the same face. The same cant to the shoulders, an old injury never healed, but so recognizable, so dear.

Anna sat, smoothing out her gown, as if it was all she'd meant to do. She put her head down on clasped hands.

Her eyes closed, she had but one thought, as urgent as prayer, over and over: *Look at me.*

She tilted her head, still on her hands, and opened her eyes.

He saw her. The intake of breath, the widening eyes revealed his recognition, and confirmed her suspicion.

Not dead. Not lost.

Restored to her.

Emotions in a flood of memories, good and sweet and sad. Suddenly, Anna had a reason to keep searching for her answers.

After the final hymn, she got up and walked away from the congregation, moving in the direction he'd indicated. She saw him vanish into a slender stand of trees by the churchyard, beyond sight of the parishioners. Slowing by the gravestones to see whether she was observed, she followed him through the late winter snow.

He was hunkered down against a tree, waiting for her. His face, like his strong hands, was older, and browned with the sun. Once they had been thought a match for each other: her blond hair fine and light, his thick and unruly. Good features on both faces, hers more precisely delicate, his kept from fae beauty by the scars of his work and weathering, but well formed, nonetheless.

Anna stepped forward. He rose and clasped her shoulders, peering into her face.

"It is you."

She nodded. "It is."

"I thought it was some dream, seeing you."

"I thought you were a thousand miles away, Bram Munroe, making your fortune. How do you come to be so close to home?"

"Ill fortune at every turn, Anna, kept me tethered here, and betrayals kept me from returning to Boston. I would not let my bad luck follow me to you."

They embraced. It started to rain, with heavy, cold drops, and she shivered. They both laughed.

"I'm a respectable widow now. There's no shame in being seen together near a warm fire." This much freedom she had, at least. The gift of a kingdom.

He nodded, but didn't move. "I'd not tarnish our meeting— a public disagreement with my former employer. A trifle, but seeing him would sour the moment."

"But . . . you are well?"

"The better for seeing you, Anna."

A shadow moving beyond the trees. Seaver, walking to the inn.

Anna collected herself; he could not have seen them. "I cannot stay. Tell me where to meet you, and I'll find you later."

"There is a shack on the dunes of the strand. Meet me there, late tonight." He pressed her hand to his lips. "Oh, Anna."

"Tonight."

For the first time in many weeks, Anna smiled.

Here, then, was what she'd been waiting for, the reason she'd continued when all seemed lost. A fresh start with an old love, plenty of money, and new ideas. No burden of her husband

Thomas Hoyt, as dead a weight alive as he was deceased. The Queen was no longer a coffin confining her; Bram and her fortune made space enough.

These happy thoughts fled as she entered the inn. Adam Seaver was sprawled out before the large fire, boots off, a pewter mug, large enough to stave in a man's head, on the table by his side. It was a cold day and there was room enough around the fire for the other patrons, but they found places away from Seaver. Perhaps they knew him, perhaps not, Anna thought. Knowing Adam Seaver was not necessary, if one had eyes to see and a brain to reason.

He seemed to sense her arrival, for he opened his eyes to slits, then sat up. "Mistress Hoyt."

There was no avoiding him now. On the ship, she'd kept to herself, pleading illness, and he had been satisfied with that.

"Mr. Seaver."

"You look very well." He stretched, and looked more closely. "Sermons agree with you."

He couldn't have seen us, she thought. She looked straight at him. "I'm glad to be off the ship."

"You'll dine with me tomorrow. We have business."

"*We* have no business. Mr. Browne asked for *you* to stop."

Seaver said nothing at this bald rebellion. Before, when he had spoken to Anna, it had been as if Mr. Browne himself had done so. He shrugged. "I would consider it a kindness, then, if you would."

There were no manners from Adam Seaver that did not conceal worse things. Anna understood she'd gone too far, too quickly. "Of course."

"I stop to collect on a debt, but the gentleman we dine with has many problems that keep him—repeatedly—from paying Mr. Browne. I admire your ability to understand people. And I know Mr. Browne does."

"I am happy to help," she said.

"Tomorrow evening, then. Across the harbor, the old tavern on Great Island." Seaver flashed a brief, broken smile, no more warm than it was lovely, and settled back to doze.

I'll help, this one last time, she thought. *Then we're done. I'll be my own woman, with the man I've always loved, and I'll have no more of you.*

She arrived at the shack after dark, her heart aloft. She carried a large jug filled with rum, and it swung heavily against her skirts. She tapped lightly on the door, and let herself in.

Bram was on her in an instant, sweeping up high, so her gown brushed the narrow walls and her hair grazed the ceiling. He stumbled, his boot causing a clank of glass bottles rolling on the tamped earth floor, and overturned the candle that lit the small room.

"Anna, Anna, 'tis the very fates bring us together now." He set her down and restored the candle carefully, with a kind of reverence, then kissed her wrists.

She found herself eager for him. With her husband, intercourse had been the price for protection. There had been no one since him, really, and she'd long ago forgotten the act might be for other than bargaining.

Later, he sighed. "You're the only one who's ever understood. No other man or woman could see me for what I am."

"Surely there've been others who've recognized your qualities."

"Never. Every time, every place, I found nothing but louts, ignorance, a desire for the mediocre. No appreciation for artistry."

"Such brilliance, to be ignored!" She put her hand on his shoulder, suppressing a smile. "They little knew they abused a lord among smiths!"

He pinched her hand playfully. "You mock me, I fear."

"I don't! I know the excellence of your hinges and bolts."

"I am Vulcan! My hammer and tongs forge miracles! The coals and heat are quick to obey me!" He laughed with her. "Drink to me now, my love!"

Tilting the jug to Anna's mouth, he sloshed the liquor over her lips. The dark spirits ran over her chin, sharp, sweet, and sticky. With his tongue, Bram traced its path across her jaw, and down her throat, burying his face in the lace at the top of her gown.

Anna shifted under him, trying to find a comfortable spot on the lumpy pallet. She sighed with happiness, intoxicated with love.

They woke in each other's arms. Bram rolled over, cradled his head, moaning, but made a brave show of it when Anna looked at him.

"It's nothing. A pounding head is a small price to pay for such a reunion."

"We'll be in Boston in two days," she said. The hopefulness that attended the thought was a sensation virtually forgotten since he'd left so abruptly five years ago. "I'll set you up there in a shop of your own."

He nodded eagerly. "It will be good to be back where I belong, back among the embers, bending metal to my will." He hesitated. "Anywhere else but Boston, though. I have enemies there."

"How so?" she said, smiling. "It's not possible. An age since you left, and all unpleasantness long forgotten, I'm sure."

"Alas, my former master—in title only!"

"Who is this man? I'll have him run out of town." She was proud to realize she had some influence now, a way to solve his problems for him.

"Bah, a bully of the first order, and he is dead, thank God. But his cousin, the one who threatened me, has a long memory. A sod the name of—Owen? Oliver. Oliver Browne."

Anna's heart seemed to stop beating for a long moment, before it resumed with a painful thump.

"But it is no matter," he continued. "We can go anywhere else, and be happy."

She thought again of her tavern. Must she choose between the Queen and Bram? There was nothing to be gained by asking aloud. Anna nodded, smiled, and dressed, and with a heavy soul and a newly aching head, she made sure no one was about as she slipped away to her room.

Had Samuel Stratton walked into the Queen's Arms, Anna would have nodded welcome, as to anyone else, and offered him one of the better chairs. Then she would have signaled her man, Josiah Ball, who handled the heavy lifting and peace-making. He would address the more volatile regulars, finding pretext to send them home. She would go about her business, pausing only to make sure the cudgel she kept behind her bar was at hand when violence broke out. Something in Stratton's carriage, and that of men like him, alerted her, like dark clouds and a drop in the barometer told of a storm. If Adam Seaver was a man to rely quietly on his reputation, retaliating privately and viciously, Samuel Stratton wore his aggression as a cloak, flourishing it at every opportunity, spoiling for trouble.

She recognized him as the man who had beaten the boy.

Stratton looked well enough—tall and hale and dark— and he seated her with a gruff and rusty courtesy. This she understood was a rarity, a gesture to Seaver's presence and Browne's influence. It extended only that far; for as soon as the tavern-keeper's wife deposited their dinner on the table and left, he ignored Anna and turned to Seaver.

"My works have been bedeviled of late. My still and stores were destroyed in the fire, and I can't supply Mr. Browne nor pay him his interest until I rebuild. If you'd convey that to him, I'd be obliged." Stratton used his knife to joint the roast bird, and then forswore cutlery as he ate the wing, using the tablecloth to wipe his fingers. "I may be delayed for months."

Seaver helped Anna to a plate of oysters, but took nothing for himself. "And the nature of this devilry?"

"Petty theft, and worse: arson and murder. My man was burned alive, trapped in the building when it went up."

Suddenly, Anna was reminded of another fire, long ago. Just before Bram had left.

"Someone has a grudge against you," Seaver said. The humor in his words suggested this was no surprise.

Stratton only grunted. "Someone will pay for it, when I find 'em." He threw the bones down, and rubbed his greasy hands together. The light in his eyes caused Anna to turn to her plate. "I think I know who it is. A little weasel I thought I could get cheap. A smith with ideas too big for him. I'll string him up by his balls, and when I'm done with him, hungry seagulls won't touch what's left."

Bram. Panic seized Anna.

"Interesting," Seaver said. "I'd like to inspect the site. I am required in Boston shortly, but I would present a full report of your troubles to Mr. Browne, and your request to—once again—delay payment."

At this invocation of Browne's name, Stratton grew less agitated, more unsure. "Thank you."

Anna and Seaver left shortly thereafter, claiming fatigue, and returned to their inn across the harbor.

"What think you of our host?" Seaver extracted his pipe and tobacco pouch.

"He lacks . . . economy. I saw him beat a boy almost to death, when he could have had the information he wanted for a piece of bread and bacon fat."

Seaver shrugged. "And the current matter?"

Anna spoke carefully, trying not to let memory—Bram's former master watching his house burn down—color her words. "He's either lying or mistaken."

"How so?"

"Thieves don't set fires; they don't want to get caught. It was an accident, or perhaps he set the fire himself, having re-moved the equipment first, to save paying what he owes Mr. Browne while secretly distilling elsewhere."

"I see." Seaver considered this. "The man killed inside?"

"Accidental or intentional, the fire covers the deed. Do you think Stratton cares about anything but his profit?"

"I think you are right, Mrs. Hoyt." He rose, and grinned. He did not truly smile, as his teeth were not made to express hap-piness. "I shall examine the place. Thank you for your opinion."

She nodded goodnight, not trusting her voice, and climbed to her room.

The door was ajar.

Her heart quickened. It mustn't be Bram, not here . . .

She rested her hand against the door, as if to discern his presence, then pushed it open.

A movement by the curtain. Anna took two steps to the table and her Bible. She picked it up, and from the recently re-paired binding withdrew a strong, slender blade. The steel was German, sharp and bright, flat for concealment in the spine of the book.

Holding it behind her skirts, she said, "Who's there? Show yourself!"

The curtains twitched again, and a bedraggled girl, barely twenty, stepped out. "Please. It's only me."

Anna knew the inn's household; this girl was no part of it. "Who are you? What are you doing here? I have no time for thieves."

"I'm Clarissa. Please . . . I need . . . Take me away from here."

A smell of molasses and charcoal and sugar burnt to acid assailed Anna's nose. "You're the one Stratton is looking for. You started the fire."

The girl straightened herself, jutted her chin out. "I didn't. I have money, I can pay my way, I just need help—"

"Money you stole." Her sureness, her lack of servility, immediately set Anna against her.

Clarissa shook her head. "My own," she said haughtily. "I stole nothing."

"Show me."

The girl unknotted a stained handkerchief. It was filled with small coins, the sort of sum accumulated with great care over a long time. A pair of new pieces of silver shone among them.

Anna took a step forward and slapped the girl twice, hard. "Those two you stole."

Clarissa's face burned, but she held Anna's stare. "It's mostly my own, with whatever was in the man's pockets. Exactly what I was owed—and if I kept the stillery running, shouldn't I have my wages? He wouldn't pay me."

"So you killed him?"

"An accident. In defense of my own person, when he tried to take advantage. And when I saw he didn't get up, I knew I'd have to leave here forever. He had no more use for the money."

"And the fire?"

"I know nothing about it, I swear."

Anna waited for the truth.

Clarissa relented. "The door opened, another man came in. I hid. I watched him pull apart the still and strike a light to a barrel of spirits. I got out as soon as I could." She shivered. "I was not certain he would ever leave, he stared at the flames so." She held out the money again. "I only need help. I can pay!"

"Why come here?"

"You stood out, on your way to church. With your fine clothes and cloak, you weren't here to stay. I thought you might need a lady's maid. And you're a stranger."

"I dined with Mr. Stratton tonight. A stranger to these parts, but not unknown."

The girl blanched. "Then let me leave."

Anna turned, and barred the door. "Sit. I may have use for you."

She glanced at Dolly, cold and mute on the table, as she reached for her Bible. She let the book fall open where it would, and began to read in Proverbs, the twentieth verse of the twenty-sixth chapter: *Where no wood is, there the fire goeth out; so where there is no talebearer, the strife ceases.*

Anna sighed and stared at Clarissa, who'd not moved all the while. She'd admitted killing Stratton's man, and had been at the fire. She had a grievance against Stratton.

Anna needed to save Bram from Stratton. She opened a trunk, studied the bottles there, selected one, and left the girl in the room, locking the door behind her.

Anna could not see for the tears in her eyes as she stumbled toward Bram's shack, splashing along the sandy shore. The salt water soaked her skirts, making them heavier and heavier, as if clutching fingers were dragging her down. The more she moved, the more difficult it became, but she slogged on until she reached the path. She sat exhausted, on a vertebra of one of the great whales they fished and slaughtered here; the place was never free of the stench. She stared at the moon, wishing it would strike her blind or remove the terrible choices before her. A few miles to the east was the wild ocean, stretching for a world away, seething, chaotic. Here, calmer waters separated her and home and all she knew too well. She sat between them to choose.

She could not hand Bram to Seaver.

She could not abandon the Queen's Arms, leave with Bram, forsake what she had. It was little enough, but hard-won and more than she'd ever dreamed of.

She thought for another hour, shivering under the moonlight. She got up heavily and walked toward the shack where Bram was sleeping. She unlatched the door, now knowing the trick of keeping it silent, and pulled it closed behind her. She watched him by the light of a guttering candle, asleep on the old pallet, snoring, as she struggled with the hooks and lacings of her sodden clothes. With patient fingers she worked; then, naked and numb, she slipped under the covers next to him.

He stirred, shuddered awake, but smiled when he saw her. "I was dreaming of you. And now you're here, conjured from the sea." He started. "You're cold as the grave—"

She put her hand on his mouth and climbed on top of him, feeling his warm body beneath her.

An hour later, when it was quiet and they could hear the wintry rain on the roof of the shed, Bram kissed Anna on the back of the neck.

In response, she reached for his hand and kissed each finger. Her lips slid down past his knuckle. He sighed, contented.

She eased the ring off his index finger, slid it onto her own, then looked into his eyes.

"I heard Samuel Stratton is looking for you. I won't let him have you. We'll run away, to New York. There's a ship tomorrow night."

He sat up. "Let us go *now*! I can find a horse—"

"No, be patient. I must keep them from you forever. Can you trust me to do that? I have a plan, and will come aboard the ship at the last minute, just before it sails."

He stared at her, then dropped his head in agreement. "Anna, you must take care. If anything should happen to you, I'd die." He held his hand over the flame of the candle, until a blister raised. "I swear it."

She hesitated, then nodded. "I understand. But you must trust me."

"With my life."

She found the bottle she'd brought with her and offered it. "Drink to it, then."

As Anna left, Bram was still and silent. She hadn't realized what hope did to a person, until this moment. Unrealistic expectation coupled with . . . something. Optimism.

It was terrible. She wept as she found her way back to her room.

The next day, Anna returned to Boston and the Queen's Arms, and found it much the same as before she'd left for London, in the care of her man Josiah. As welcome as its familiarity was, the tavern's walls seemed to press in around her, leaving her breathless.

All was well, but not yet to her liking.

If she had given up Bram, not willing to relinquish the small fortune and cupful of power she'd carefully amassed, neither was she ready to return to drawing beer and measuring rum. By choosing to thwart Browne and Seaver and Stratton, she'd chosen more.

There was no certainty in life. She'd learned the power

of social barriers in London, but she'd also learned how laws could be winked at, and yet public esteem maintained, by the respectable whore in the Eastham church.

So *more* it must be, and by her will, rather than *certainty*.

But carefully, carefully. She would never be free of Browne and Seaver, but she might learn to work . . . in their margins. Alongside them, if not beneath them.

In the next days, she went to the merchant Rowe about the purchase of a piece of his land outside the city. They shook hands after negotiating; he had a faint smile on his face. Hers was quite determined. It would be the first of many such purchases she'd make. She had plans of her own now.

She sat at her desk, entered the transaction in her ledger, then drafted a note to the lawyer Clark, giving him instructions about the purchase and asking him to find a secondhand copper still for her. She considered who she would employ in her future enterprises and drew a list. It was short, but every one reliable.

There was a knock at her door; the taproom boy was there, announcing a visitor. His eyes were wide.

Seaver? It might be a short career, then, if he discovered her betrayal. She looked to the little blond manikin and asked, "Dolly, what is the right lie?"

The caller was Clarissa.

The girl looked much better for a change of air and a change of dress. Fresh-scrubbed and the gray under her eyes replaced with roses, she was the picture of modesty. Better, she was unrecognizable, even in Anna's blue velvet cloak.

"Mr. Munroe took my absence well?" Anna asked.

Clarissa laughed.

Anna shrugged, surprised at how little she felt now, only glad her plan worked. "But he won't be back?"

"Oh, no. He won't dare come to Boston, now that he believes you left his ring at the site of the fire for Mr. Seaver and Mr. Stratton to find. He cursed you, roundly and foully. Even threatened to kill you—I wasn't sure I'd escape his rage—but the money you paid the captain was enough to keep him on board, while I slipped back ashore. He won't show himself here."

Anna nodded, trying not to look at her battered Bible. There was a slight gap between the pages in the middle, where she'd hidden Bram's ring. "*Where no wood is, there the fire goeth out.*"

"What's that?"

"From Proverbs. You can read?"

Clarissa nodded.

Anna hesitated. The girl owed her much and was clever enough. Perhaps she would do.

"Start with this, then." She handed Clarissa a new Bible. "You'll need to read, if you're to work for me, and you'll find many answers here."

NINETEEN SNAPSHOTS OF DENNISPORT

BY PAUL TREMBLAY

Dennisport

1.

That's me standing on the porch of the summer house we always rented. I drove by the old place today. Sunset Lane, just off Depot Street. The house still has that aqua-green paint job. Four other summer houses crowd around it, almost like they're boxing it in, or protecting it. I don't remember those other houses being so close, taking up the whole lane. Everything seemed bigger back then.

Look at me. Hard to believe how skinny and little I was. She's not in the shot, but my sister Liz, who was one year younger, towered over me, and probably outweighed me by a solid twenty pounds. Would you just look at that kid? Those legs are skinnier and whiter than the porch slats. This was, what, 1986, so I'd just turned thirteen. It's the first picture on that vacation roll. I always had to be in the first picture by myself. It was my thing.

2.

That's my mother carrying the towels. She already looks aggravated. I would've been too. None of us kids helped to unpack. The other woman is her younger sister, my Aunt Christine. She was my coolest aunt. She lived in Boston and always liked to play games or take us kids to the movies. I think that's an emergency rainy-day puzzle box tucked under her arm. Aunt

Christine and my parents were in their mid-thirties. Jesus, everyone was so young. People don't do that anymore, do they? Have kids so young.

My cheap camera makes everyone look so far away. It broke before the end of the summer. That group of people running away, on the right side of the house, they're hard to make out, but that's my younger brother, Ronnie, slung over my dad's shoulder. He stole Dad's floppy Budweiser hat and tried to make a quick escape. You can kind of see the hat bunched up in one hand. Ronnie was eight and built like a hobbit. Liz was tickling Ronnie, trying to help Dad. She always took his side over ours.

3.

Here's Ronnie and his summer buzz cut, standing in a big sand pit we spent most of the day digging. Can't really tell in the picture, but he had this white patch of hair on the right side of his head. Buzzed that short, it looked like the map of some island country.

The sand at the bottom of that pit was shockingly wet and cold. I couldn't admit it to Ronnie, but we got to a point where I didn't want to reach down to dig anymore. I was a big scaredy cat. Always was, especially compared to Ronnie.

We're on one of those Nantucket Sound beaches off Old Wharf Road. I remember the road as a long string of nameless hotels and motels and restaurants and beaches fitting together, squares on a chessboard. In this picture, we're at the public beach next to what's now called the Edgewater Beach Resort. I don't remember what was there back then. Isn't that terrible? So many of the little details always go missing. Maybe if I hadn't been so preoccupied with taking pictures, I would've remembered more.

Check this out: I caught it by accident, but those legs

there, upper right corner, those are my dad's legs. He was following Aunt Christine to the water, but then he stopped to talk to some big guy wearing long pants, shoes, and a yellow shirt. The yellow shirt I remember vividly. I didn't get a great look at him otherwise, but I remember him being bigger and older than my dad.

I asked Ronnie who Dad was talking to. Ronnie didn't know. We waited for Dad to come back, we wanted to bury him in the pit since it was too deep for either one of us. When he got back and we asked who he was talking to, he said, "Just some guy." We were all used to Dad talking to random people: grocery store, baseball game, walking down the street, didn't matter to him. Used to embarrass the hell out of us (especially Liz). Talking to strangers and getting them to laugh or at least smile was what he did.

Ronnie and I tried to sneak up behind Dad and push him into the pit. He threw us in instead. I knocked heads with Ronnie. We were fine, but I got real mad at my father, mad like only a new teenager can. Dad didn't care. He held us down and buried us in the sand.

4.

Rainy-day picture. The choice was go with Dad, who went off by himself to pick up groceries, or stay in the house and work on a puzzle with everyone else. I stayed. I hated puzzles, but I sat and listened to Def Leppard and the Scorpions on my Walkman.

No one really likes puzzles. Mom, Aunt Christine, Liz, and Ronnie don't look excited or happy. You can tell by the way Mom has her arms crossed and is turned away from the table. They were all out of patience and annoyed with each other.

That's how I remember puzzles ending: nothing getting solved and people walking away muttering to themselves.

5.

Here we are playing wiffle ball with the boys who stayed in the house next to us. I don't remember their names. They were from Jersey. The tall redhead was my age and had terrible acne. Looked like his skin hurt all the time. The short redhead was a couple of years older than Ronnie, had round Mr. Peabody glasses, and his face was full of freckles. They were geekier than I was, which is saying something. Back home, kids at school and in the neighborhood picked on me a lot, and I never said boo. But Dennisport wasn't home, it was somewhere else, and I became the de facto leader of our little summer group: me, my brother (Liz wouldn't be seen with any of us), the Jersey Reds.

The first couple of days, we tried following around this girl from Italy, Isabella. Her name I remember. She was only twelve, maybe even eleven, but she looked older than me. She didn't speak any English, had curly light brown hair down to her butt, and wore short-shorts with white trim. She tolerated us for a bit, but ended up hanging around with a group of kids older than us.

When we weren't following Isabella around, we spied on my father.

6.

Yeah, I took a picture of my hand holding a glass bottle of Coke. There was this small motel down Old Wharf, right before one of the public beaches, that had an antique Coke vending machine. It was expensive, and the bottles held less than cans, but I was convinced Coke tasted better in glass bottle form.

It was down here at the vending machine where we first started spying on my father. Ronnie saw him walking across the sand-filled motel parking lot. Him in his thick black beard, already tan, and muscular in a wiry kind of way. I used to obsess over how different I was from my father.

Us kids instinctively ducked behind a parked car, wordlessly deciding we were going to jump out and scare Dad or try and tackle him into some nearby sand dune. No way the four of us could've taken him.

He didn't walk by us, though. He veered off toward a set of motel rooms. He stopped seemingly at random and knocked on a blue door. The door opened and he went inside. No greeting or anything, he just went in and the door shut behind him.

Spying on your dad is a younger kid's game. But being on vacation, away from home like that, away from who you were (particularly if you didn't like who you were), was like permission to act younger than ourselves. Unless Isabella was around, of course.

So we tried waiting Dad out, but he didn't walk back through that blue door. We got bored and went to the beach.

7.

Ronnie took this picture without me knowing. The younger Jersey Red said that maybe my Dad was cheating on my mother with the motel maid. So I jumped him, and put him in this headlock and forced him into the water. I remember not feeling all that strong, but he let me hold on and give him his fair share of noogies.

8.

That's the same Coke-bottle motel. Early the next morning, Dad said he was going out for a jog. Ronnie and I followed him. We both stayed quiet, taking this much more seriously than the game it supposedly was.

I tried getting a shot with the blue door open, hoping I could see who was behind it, but clearly I failed. I mean, it's partially open and when I first got this picture developed, if you looked hard enough, you could see the ghost of my father's shoulder disappearing in the shadow of the room. But you can't see it anymore.

9.

We're in a record store in downtown Yarmouth. That's a picture of the wall of T-shirts, and the Scorpions one in the middle that I couldn't buy. I'd already spent my money on a Sandy Koufax baseball card at the shop next door. It wasn't his rookie year card, but a 1962 Topps that was still pretty sweet.

That afternoon was kind of a slog through the gift shops and kitsch stores. We tried to be good little tourists. It was hot, the streets were crowded, and other than the candy store (where I filled up on saltwater taffy and Nerds), we all wanted to go different places. I fought with Liz who didn't want to go anywhere. Mom and Dad fought over where to eat. You could tell Aunt Christine was pissed, because she took Ronnie off on her own. Then Liz and Mom, arguing with each other but quietly at least, went off. I went with Dad to the baseball card store, then the record store, and Dad wouldn't buy me anything.

When we all met back up later, Ronnie was smiling and carrying monster-movie posters. The kid was taunting me with them. I whined to Dad about how come he wouldn't buy me a lousy T-shirt. Dad asked how old I was in a way that made everyone go quiet.

~~10.~~

I moved this picture to the end of the album. Notice how the empty rectangle of space is a darker shade of green compared to the rest of the page. It's ironic that the original or true color of the page was preserved by the photo, preserved by that piece of the past.

11.

This one's blurry because Ronnie hit my elbow as I was taking the shot of the movie marquee. He did it on purpose. I punched him in the shoulder and almost went at it with him right there in line. We were on edge because we were both nervous about how scary the movie was going to be. At least, I was on edge. Ronnie had seen tons of horror movies on cable but this was going to be his first in a theater. He didn't say much as a kid, but he'd been talking about seeing this movie all day long.

Dad and Aunt Christine took us to see the remake of *The Fly*. Mom stayed home by herself and played solitaire. She said she didn't like horror movies, but she'd been staying back at the house by herself a lot that vacation.

I arranged it so Liz sat on the aisle, then Ronnie, me, Dad, and Aunt Christine. During the movie Liz and Ronnie whispered jokes to each other, and Dad and Aunt Christine did the same. I hugged my knees to my chest and white-knuckled the whole flick. The slow and inexorable transformation of nice-guy mad-scientist Jeff Goldblum into Brundlefly was terrifying, revolting, and sad in a way I couldn't explain. I'd sneak peeks at Dad to make sure he wasn't changing, wasn't melting before my eyes, that he looked like he was supposed to.

Then there was that gross end scene, where Brundlefly vomits up his digestive enzymes on the guy's hand and melts it. Man, I lost my breath, and my legs started moving like I was going to up and run out of the theater.

I looked away and watched Dad watching the movie instead. During the screams and other violent sounds of Brundlefly's demise, I almost asked Dad who he was seeing in that motel.

12.

On Main Street, not too far from our rental, near the intersection of Routes 28 and 134, there was a pocket of kiddie
places: an ice cream shack, an old bumper car place, and a
trampoline fun park. It was just me, Ronnie, and Dad. The
trampolines were sunk into the ground, surrounded by gravel.
When you landed it felt like you were shrinking, or melting
away like Brundlefly.

This is a picture of the parking lot at the bumper car place.
We did the bumpers before ice cream, but after trampolines.
Everyone, even people I didn't know, would drive their bumper cars into Dad because he was laughing the loudest, calling
people out, being a goof. Like I said, everyone loved him.

Ronnie and I got back in line for a second and third go-
round on the bumpers. Dad went out to the parking lot. I
couldn't follow him outside without being too obvious. Instead, from the bumper car line, I tried to get a shot of him.
I couldn't see who he was with, but I heard him talking. All
you can see here is a screen window, and some cars in the lot.
There was a better view of the lot from the bumper car floor,
but every time I was close to seeing who he was talking to, I got
blindsided, usually by Ronnie.

13.

This is a picture of the first and only summer group meeting I
called in my bedroom. It's a good action shot. That white blur
there is the pillow I threw at the Jersey Reds before snapping
the picture.

We started off talking about music. They liked rap, which
was typical Jersey, right? Then we talked about Isabella and
trying to get her to come with us to the ice cream place on Sea
Street. Then we talked about girlfriends back home. None of
us had any, although in a fit of personal confession that was

clearly out of place, I admitted to having a terrible, hopeless crush on a girl named J.J. Katz. The Jersey Reds thought that was the funniest thing they'd ever heard and spent ten minutes shouting *dyn-o-mite* like the guy from the TV show *Good Times*. I kind of lost my status as the leader of the group right there.

Then we talked about our theories of what my father was up to. When I say we, I'm not including Ronnie. He just sat there and didn't say a word. Most of what was said wasn't serious and was part of the game, Dad-as-secret-agent-man kind of stuff, until I opened my yap and was again too honest for the moment, too honest for the room. I told them how my father would bet on football in the fall, how he'd bring home from work what he called his football cards. They were white rectangles of cardboard, printed with a list of teams and point spreads. He'd pick four teams, or ten teams, or both, and sometimes he'd let me pick a few of them for him.

I didn't really know anything about what was happening with Dad, but I think it sounded like I did.

I remember almost telling them about a few months before that vacation, when I was upstairs listening to my parents argue in the kitchen, Dad saying, "It'll be okay," and, "I'm sorry," and Mom too hysterical to understand, until she screamed, "Fuck you," ran out of the kitchen, and kicked out one of the small plate-glass windows in the front door.

The younger Jersey Red started in again with his your-father-is-hooking-up-with-another-woman theory. He said my father looked like the kind of guy who could get women to go to a hotel with him. Ronnie still didn't say anything, but I could tell he was upset. To be honest, I was kind of proud that my dad looked like that kind of guy, and that it somehow meant I was cooler.

I held out my camera and told the Reds that I had evidence and that it wasn't my dad with some other girl. They asked if I had any pictures of *dyn-o-mite* J.J. on my camera. That's when I threw the pillow and took the picture.

14.

Dad came home from a morning jog with a black eye. He laughed and said he slid on some sand, fell, and hit his face off a duck-shaped mailbox. I was surprised he let me take this picture. I don't think he wanted me to, but what could he say or do with the rest of the family there in the kitchen, pointing and laughing at him?

15.

All right, that's a picture of the girl from Italy, Isabella, walking away and waving at us. We'd tracked her down and asked her if she wanted to go for ice cream. She pretended not to understand what we were asking despite the Jersey Reds' embarrassing ice cream pantomime. Which was fine. I got a picture anyway.

16.

There's a time gap here with the pictures. I can't remember if there were more photos and I lost them, or if I didn't take them. Sometimes I wonder how much of this I would remember if there were no photos, no proof.

Here we are eating breakfast at the Egg and I. Everyone looks haggard and frazzled because there were only a few days left to the vacation. The Jersey Reds were gone. It was just us. We were all fighting and annoying each other. And again, maybe it's only the lens of elapsed time making it all clearer, but we were all on edge. Something was going on with Dad but no one knew what, and no one was talking about it.

Aunt Christine and Mom are looking away from the camera and away from each other. Mom might be staring at the ashtray she has filled. Liz has her hand in front of her face, and Ronnie, never quite the exhibitionist anyway, his face is a blank. He'd been like that since the morning of Dad's black eye, which was the same morning I told him about the big fight back home and Mom kicking the window out.

They're pissed off at me for taking a stupid picture of the table. Or maybe they were all thinking about Dad, and asking themselves why he had to make a call from the pay phone three booths over.

17.

Check out this shot. This was the small private beach for our little Depot Street/Sunset Lane association, a patch of steeply sloped sand next to the big Ocean House restaurant. When it was high tide, it wasn't even really a beach, more like a dune, or a cliff of sand. I went to that beach today and I don't know if it's because of erosion or my memory exaggerating everything, but there's barely a discernable slope there now.

Ronnie spent our second-to-last day of vacation running and jumping off the steep slope, catching major air, and crashing knee-deep into the sand at the bottom. He jumped so much, he had raspberries on his legs after.

I did it with him a few times, but the landing hurt my ankles. It was too steep. I went off to the side and climbed the base of a rock jetty, and asked what he thought was going on with Dad. He said, "I don't know." I asked if he was going to get up wicked early with me to follow him on his jog. He said, "I don't know." That was it. He jumped, climbed back up, and jumped.

This is a great shot of Ronnie in mid-jump, arms extended behind him, feet out in front, eyes closed. You look at this long enough, you start to expect him to land.

18.

There isn't much to see in this one, right? Too dark.

I woke up to the sound of the front screen door shutting. It bounced in the frame, hinges squeaking. That door is still squeaking as far as I'm concerned. It was dark out, but I didn't look at a clock, didn't wake Ronnie or anyone else. Just threw on my sneakers, grabbed my camera off the nightstand, and ran outside.

It was a cloudy night, and I couldn't see the moon or any stars. I didn't see Dad anywhere, and I was worried that I'd been too slow. The streets were empty, and so were the beaches and the restaurant parking lots. I headed toward the Coke-bottle motel and didn't see him there either. But that room he usually went to, the motel door was wide open, and inside the lights were off. I ran as quietly as I could across Old Wharf, then through the parking lot to another section of the motel just to the right of the open door. I crept up to it with my back pressed against the motel wall, camera held out. I was going to walk by the open door, snap a picture, and bolt.

Then I heard something. It sounded far away, like it had been carried in by the ocean. It was someone crying. I knew it was Dad, even if I'd never heard him like that before.

I ran to the motel beach but didn't see anything, so I worked my way back to the Ocean House, and to our little private beach with its steep slope and rock jetty. I ducked behind the jetty as I found him. Only he wasn't alone. Another man was leading him into the water.

It was too dark to see details, but I think there was a bag over Dad's head. The other guy had something in his hand, a gun maybe. I don't know. It was low tide, and they were walking way out there, past the jetty already, but only waist-deep in water.

I didn't know what to do, so I took a picture. I don't know if either of them saw the flash.

I didn't see the end either. It was too dark and they were too far out. Only the other man came back to the beach. I ducked behind the jetty again. He walked by, just a few feet away, on the other side of the rocks. I heard him breathing heavily.

I don't remember the rest of the night. Don't remember if I went to the beach to look for Dad. Don't remember how long I stayed huddled behind the jetty and don't remember walking back to the house and crawling into bed next to Ronnie. That was where I woke the next morning. I didn't tell anyone what I saw. I was in shock. I was only thirteen years old.

Two days later, his body washed up on shore. All the stories in the papers were about a tourist drowning on a late-night swim.

After we were home, after the funeral, when I picked up my developed pictures, I thought I'd go to the police, tell them everything, show them everything. But the pictures didn't show anything, really, and too much time had passed. I was still afraid, and to be honest, I was mad at my father, mad that he'd let something like that happen to him.

So, this picture. There isn't much to see in it, right? Too dark. When I looked at this—and I looked at this for years and years, every night before I went to bed, like the first picture of the motel room door I showed you—I thought if I looked hard enough, I could see him there. But you can only make out black water, the outline of the beach and the jetty. Nothing else. You can't see anything.

There's another picture I've been staring at for years too.

10.

This is what I moved to the last page. I took this after the record store, but before we all met back up again, so it was just me and Dad. A random picture of my father on the sidewalk of downtown Yarmouth, right? Look closer. Over his left shoulder. See that huge guy two storefronts away, hiding under an awning, but not hiding. He's watching behind reflective sunglasses, and he's wearing a tight white polo shirt, wearing it like a threat, wearing it the same way he wore that yellow shirt. That's the same yellow-shirt guy from the beach Dad was talking to on our first day of vacation.

I've been staring at this picture of you for almost twenty-five years, a quarter of a century. It's hard to understand how all that time passed so quickly. In many ways, I'm still that kid cowering behind the jetty. In other ways, I'm not.

The funny thing is, I never planned for this. It's not like I've been searching for you all this time. I wasn't even looking for you when I saw you.

19.

The thing of it is, I don't even want to know why you did what you did. It does and it doesn't matter. In any case, it's not that hard to figure out. And sure, a few years ago I asked my mother about the big fight I'd heard and why she kicked out the window on the front door. She said that Dad had blown four grand to a bookie. Four grand was a lot of money in 1986, right? Sure it was.

You see this camera? It used to belong to my grandfather. You're probably about the same age he was when he died. Anyway, I kept the camera in working condition. Do you remember Polaroids? I'm sure you do. I'm sure you remember lots of things.

So this is you, duct taped to a chair in our hotel room. It's hard to see with the tape over your mouth, the bruises, the dried blood, but it's you. I know, compared to the you in the other picture, this you is the Brundlefly. But this was and is you, even if you are so much smaller than you used to be.

I've brought you back down to Dennisport. Just like old times, right? We're at the Sea Shell Motel next to the Ocean House. I put the room on your card but don't worry, it's off-season, so I got a great rate.

This is the last picture on the last page of my album. I took this picture while you weren't awake. Even for someone of your advanced age, you sure do sleep a lot.

I'm not one hundred percent sure what I want out of this. I could just leave you here and go back home to my own young family. Maybe you'd call the police or come after me yourself, or come after me with a little help. Maybe you wouldn't do anything. Maybe everything would be okay if I just unwrapped you and watched you weakly limp out of here, old man that you are, and more than just a little broken. That might be enough for me.

Maybe later tonight, I'll take you by the hand, the one that's shaking even now when it's taped behind your back, and we'll take a walk together out into the water, the very same water. But it's not the same water, it's different. Maybe that's okay.

So maybe we'll walk out there, past the jetty, up to our waists in water, and just stand there and feel the cold all around us. Then maybe, at the very least, you'll admit who you are and what you did to him and what you did to me.

VARIATIONS ON A FIFTY-POUND BALE

by Adam Mansbach
Martha's Vineyard

I t is generally agreed upon that at some point during the last several decades, a fifty-pound bale of commercial-grade marijuana, sealed in plastic and lashed with burlap, was found bobbing no more than a thousand feet off Menemsha Beach, in the calm waters separating Martha's Vineyard from the privately owned, unpopulated Elizabeth Islands.

No consensus is to be had regarding the discoverer of this child-sized brick (child-sized in the sense of weighing as much as a ten-year-old, not in the sense of being an appropriate portion for a preadolescent), nor its fate. The consistency with which otherwise divergent tales pinpoint the size and location suggest a singular event, much as the persistence of flood myths across the whole of the world's indigenous cultures is taken as evidence that some such cataclysm did occur. The bale is never forty pounds, or sixty; it is never found floating off Lucy Vincent Beach in Chilmark by nudist Jews, or spotted undulating in the frothy surf of Edgartown's South Beach by salmon trouser–clad Republicans.

No version accounts for how a solitary swimmer—it is always a solitary swimmer, and the bale is always sighted from the beach, never a boat—managed to maneuver this ottoman-shaped prize back to the island's most public beach without attracting the kind of attention he would doubtlessly seek to avoid.

There are two possibilities. One is that the bale was not spotted during the summer months, and thus the beach was deserted, the boat slips empty, the Hatfield-and-McCoy blood-feuding fish stores closed. Launching oneself into the ocean in the dead of winter or the dying of fall would have required far greater curiosity or bravery or foolishness or intuition on the part of the swimmer, or else previous experience in large-scale drug trafficking. Perhaps he had one of those. Perhaps he had several.

But if it was summer—as seems likely, that being when people go to the beach—the swimmer would have decided to come ashore somewhere more private. Menemsha Beach ends a few hundred yards east, past a stone jetty. The coastline bunches, like a piece of fabric caught in a sewing machine, and all the land is private. Probably, the swimmer found an inlet or a dock, stashed his bale, and came back for it later with a car. Presumably, the teenage lifeguard on duty was too busy flirting or applying zinc oxide to his nose to notice any of this, or he didn't care, or he was a friend of the swimmer's and it was his car in which the bale rode home. Or else the swimmer was the lifeguard himself, which would make a lot of sense: binoculars, elevated chair, nautical aptitude.

It is also possible that it was simply 1973 when all this happened, and nobody raised an eyebrow at a bale of weed, so the swimmer just hauled it straight up onto the sand, where everybody slapped him on the back and said things like "Far out, man," and grabbed fistfuls to take home.

In one popular version of the story, the guy—let's call him Zonk—decides the best way to maximize profits (or the only way to make any sales) is to move the load piecemeal, small-bore, eighth-ounces, quarters, dime bags. Who cares how long it takes? Hell, the longer the better so long as it means he doesn't have to work.

Zonk is an islander, knows everybody, does a little carpentry and a little fishing and plays guitar in a bar band just like fifty or a hundred other still-young-but-getting-older catch-as-catch-can good-time Island Charlies. It's the 1970s, and Zonk's got a beat-to-shit Ford pickup he tools around in, only it's broken at the moment, needs a new fan belt, so he's been hitching. Luckily, the mechanics at Up-Island Garage are all stoners, so by the weekend Zonk is up and running. He throws the whole bale into the flatbed, ties it down with a tarp, and spends the next few days making the rounds, *howdy friends and acquaintances, I come bearing sensi,* like he's the Good Humor Man or something.

A few buddies tell Zonk he's insane to roll around with the entire load like that, but their warnings are drowned out by the silent approval of the majority. Back then, not only do most Vineyarders not lock their cars, they never even remove their keys from the ignition. Granted, the example is flawed, as few things are less tenable than stealing a car on an island. The point is, there's a pervasive atmosphere of trust. Which is not to say that Zonk isn't something of a dipshit.

These days, Brazilians do all the Vineyard's landscaping, and half the construction; most avoid driving except in a company vehicle, because they're undocumented and if they get pulled over, they could end up on an airplane. The cops know they're here, of course, and for the most part, it's a live-and-let-live landscape, since the island would fall apart without them, but a traffic violation could still bring everything tumbling down. Before the Brazilians, it was Eastern European college kids coming over for the summer to work the cash registers and clean the hotel rooms, Slovaks and Ukrainians and Poles, plus a sprinkling of Jamaicans. But if you rewind all the way to Zonk's Summer of Bud, the migrant seasonal help is all Irish and predominantly teenage. A lot of them stay together in a kind of barracks out by the airport, long gone now and prob-ably doomed from the moment a building inspector got around to visiting.

The Irish kids come back year after year, trading up from retail to construction as their muscles come in. They bring their cousins, and sometimes their sisters and sweethearts. The girls post colorful, handmade fliers at the Chilmark Com-munity Center and the six town libraries, advertising them-selves as au pairs and mothers' helpers, and make more money than the boys. There is usually a tapped keg of Natural Light or Milwaukee's Best at the barracks, sitting in a plastic trash can full of ice. If a few of the boys are able to get three days off in a row, they take the ferry to Woods Hole and the bus to Bos-ton, which they call "Southie," and return with new tattoos.

Sometimes they turn up at islander parties, but the Irish kids make guys like Zonk uncomfortable. There is a sense of menace to them, as if bone-shattering violence is always only another beer away, and what makes it worse is that you can't be certain you aren't just imagining it. The Irish boys seem to know what they're doing. Who they're supposed to become.

Zonk figures they'll buy an assload of weed from him, and he is right. The barracks pools its resources, and Zonk lets the McDonnell brothers, Sean and James, chisel him down a hun-dred bucks on a quarter-pound—more than twice the amount he's sold to date. He stands there in the middle of the woods with them from early sunset to pitch black, drinking beers and listening to stories about crippling rugby injuries they've wit-nessed and inflicted, then gets back in his truck and motors home to take a nap before the night cranks up.

It's worth noting that the McDonnell brothers feature in any number of stories, usually as black hat–wearing villains or entropy-embodying Billy Badasses, and that police records from the era reflect no such thing. Sean was arrested four times between 1976 and 1979, twice for disorderly conduct, once for misdemeanor theft, and once for assault. James's record includes a DUI, an underage drinking charge, and an assault rap. Neither served any time. Not in Massachusetts, anyway.

Zonk wakes up, scarfs down a leftover thing of clam chowder, and makes his way to a small gathering in the town now called Aquinnah and then known as Gay Head. Only when he's parked, climbed up on the Ford's flatbed, and thrown off the tarp to grab some nugs for smoking and selling does he realize his stash is gone.

There are a couple of Irish au pairs from the barracks there, the kind of cute, frisky fifteen-year-olds who always move as a duo and only last one summer on the Vineyard because the older brothers or cousins who've brought them spend all their time engaged in a furious and losing battle to defend the girls' purity. Zonk and a few of his bearded fishermen-carpenter compatriots corner them and demand, wild-eyed, to know where Sean and James are.

The girls shrug and tilt their beer cans to their lips, then call over two more fifteen-year-old au pairs. Eventually, it emerges that the McDonnell brothers have their boss's Jeep for the weekend, and are on their way to Southie.

Zonk, or somebody acting on Zonk's behalf, calls the Vineyard Haven cops and tells them a red Laredo containing two Irishmen and fifty pounds of marijuana is either boarding the last Woods Hole–bound ferry or has recently reached the mainland and is currently headed north on Route 24.

The cops call the Steamship Authority, learn the ship has left the port. The man who answers the on-board phone, a ferry worker whose name is lost to history or bullshit, is appraised of the situation, asked to confirm the presence of a red Laredo registered to the Tisbury Landscaping & Construction

Co., and told to sit tight; the Woods Hole PD will meet the boat and take it from there.

Sensing an opportunity for heroism or grand larceny, the ferry worker unlocks the safebox in the crew quarters, removes and loads the handgun stored there, and makes his way to the cargo bay. There, he finds the Laredo. And the McDonnell brothers, slumped down in the front bucket seats, passing a pint of whiskey.

The ferry worker's approach lacks artifice. Glancing behind him in the driver's-side mirror, Sean sees a man snaking through the narrow aisle between vehicles with a gun held low at his side. The McDonnell brothers jump from the doorless Jeep and rush him. No shots are fired; whatever the ferry worker has in mind, he does not have in body. It is also possible that the gun jammed.

Either way, Sean and James McDonnell beat the nameless ferry worker within a yard of his life, and then they either do or do not throw him off the boat into the blue-black moonlit or not-moonlit Atlantic. There is no record of a ferry worker dying, so if they throw him off, he swims. It is even possible, if slightly romantic, to imagine Sean and James providing him with a life vest or an instantly inflating raft, both of which are in ample and accessible supply.

Regardless of how the McDonnell brothers dispense with the ferry worker, it does not solve the problem they now understand themselves to be confronting: namely, that the authorities know what is in the Jeep, and Sean and James are trapped in the middle of the ocean.

Thinking quickly, the brothers do one of three things.

They decide to cut their losses, *easy come easy go*, and heave the contraband into the water. This possibility is attractive in that it returns the bale of weed to the ocean from whence it came, setting the stage for rediscovery and further adventures.

It is even conceivable that the ferry worker, if he too is in the drink, finds the bale and paddles it to shore.

Or else, the McDonnell brothers figure *in for a dime, in for a dollar*, steal a lifeboat, and load the bale. Then one of them rows home and stashes the shit, denying the limp-dick accusations of Zonk and his weirdo-beardo islander pals, while the other stays with the Jeep, drives it off the docks, and sits placidly on the nearest curb in handcuffs as the WHPD search it to no avail, eventually accepting the baffled officers' apologies and heading up to Southie.

Or perhaps, and most ingeniously, Sean and James transfer the bale to another vehicle—the flatbed of a truck, perhaps—and one of the brothers stows away there also, with the ferry worker's gun. WHPD surround the disembarking Jeep and find nothing; meanwhile, some working stiff drives the bale and the hidden McDonnell brother onto the mainland, then is ordered at gunpoint to deliver both to a prearranged rendezvous point, such as the parking lot of the International House of Pancakes just before the Bourne Bridge.

Another equally apocryphal story takes place in the late 1960s. The swimmer—let's call him Timothy—is a staid, respectable type in his mid-thirties. He and his wife, both professors at a small liberal arts college somewhere in northern New England, have been renting the same Vineyard Haven house each summer for six or seven years.

Timothy is no drug dealer, but he's no fool, either. Sitting in his basement, staring at this absurd quantity of marijuana, he knows the only sensible thing to do is sell it all at once, as quickly as possible and at an attractive markdown.

Timothy does not move among the exceedingly wealthy, especially not the kind of rich people likely to drop fifty thousand dollars (Timothy's steep-discount appraisal of the bale's market value) on reefer. But the exceedingly wealthy are certainly within shouting distance, here on Martha's Vineyard in glorious mid-August, and they are full of surprises. Why wouldn't one of them want to lay in a supply of cannabis? The thing to do, Timothy decides, is to proceed as he would were it a barrel of Chateau Mouton Rothschild 1945 he'd pulled out of the surf. Only with greater discretion.

Timothy waits a couple of days, then begins making quiet, theoretically phrased inquiries at the cocktail parties he and his wife attend at the rate of two per night. On consecutive evenings, multiple interlocutors invoke the same man as a potential buyer, and here the story trifurcates.

The enthusiast is either a foreign-born energy magnate who owns a palatial spread in Chilmark, a best-selling novelist with harbor-front property in Vineyard Haven, or a glaucoma-stricken movie star retired to a hundred-acre farm in West Tisbury.

No telling of the story specifies how Timothy manages to secure entrée to the tycoon, writer, or actor—although presumably, as an enthusiastic and pedigreed cocktail party–goer on a miniscule and rarefied island, he is separated from these distinguished personages by no more than one or two degrees.

Trundling his product in a pair of smart new suitcases, Timothy is shown into the Chilmark, Vineyard Haven, or West Tisbury estate sometime around eleven at night, by a servant. A large dinner party seems to have recently adjourned. Timothy is unsure what to do, but the servant—assistant is probably a better word—makes it all very easy. He relieves Timothy of the bags, hands him a personal check for fifty thousand dollars, and asks if he has time to stay for a drink. Timothy says he does, and is shown to a screened porch or den in which half a dozen men are sipping bourbon and smoking cigars.

The actor or writer or tycoon greets Timothy warmly, fixes

him a drink, and insists that he tell the story of his windfall. But Timothy finds himself tongue-tied, because among the men who break off talking and turn toward him with an air of inquiry is Frank Sinatra.

Timothy is not starstruck. He is terrified. He has read about Sinatra. He knows the Chairman of the Board is a Mafioso, mixed up with the gangsters who got Kennedy killed. He does not belong in a room with this man—this man and his muscle. For that is what the others are, Timothy realizes at once: the singer's portable amen corner of New Jersey *paisanos*, every last one decked out in a gorgeous handmade suit slightly inferior to Il Padrone's.

A few beats of silence is all it takes for Sinatra to lose interest in Timothy, and when his attention flags, so does that of every other man in the room. Timothy is merely an observer now, and by the time his panic subsides, Sinatra is holding forth on cigars, waving his in the air so that the ember draws a streak of light and telling the star or writer or businessman that what he needs instead of this second-rate crap are some authentic hand-rolled Cubans.

Sinatra drains his glass. It is instantly refilled. He takes it down to half-mast, then calls for a telephone, announcing that he's going to procure some decent shit.

"Who you gonna call, Frank?" the host asks, chuckling.

"Who the hell do you think?"

A phone is placed on the low table before him.

Sinatra lifts the receiver, dials a zero.

"Hello, sweetheart. I'd like to place a long-distance call.

"Havana, Cuba.

"Mr. Fidel Castro.

"Tell him it's Frank. Sinatra."

Nothing else of Timothy's evening survives to be retold. Sometime the following week, he buys a house in Oak Bluffs, paying forty thousand dollars in cash and taking occupancy the same day. By some accounts, he and his wife have been summering quietly there ever since. By others, the man whose marijuana Timothy brought ashore turns up that weekend. Let's call him Blackbeard.

Blackbeard is a grizzled old cutthroat from Nova Scotia, a commercial fisherman who's spent a lifetime trawling the corridors of the Atlantic, the Caribbean—hell, it's all one ocean when you come down to it, he says, grinning at Timothy and turning to share the sunshine with the towering, snaggletoothed colleague standing by his side, forearms crossed over a whiskey-barrel chest.

With no further preamble, Blackbeard comes to his point. There was some inclement weather on his last voyage north, he says, spreading his hands, and also some . . . let's call it human error. A few pieces of cargo were lost. Word down at the docks is that one of those pieces found its way to land, and into the hands of—

He breaks off, laughs, and tells Timothy that he can probably guess the rest. Blackbeard is here to reclaim his property, and offer Timothy a small finder's fee.

Timothy, to his surprise, finds that he is not nearly as frightened, standing at his new threshold with two seafaring drug-smugglers, as he was in the presence of Frank Sinatra. His breath remains regular. He shoves his hands into his pockets, and tells the truth.

"I sold it and bought this house."

Blackbeard does not take the news in stride. He demands to be reimbursed in cash or cargo, and makes clear that his still-unintroduced colleague is conversant in the art of breaking legs.

Still, Timothy does not panic. He asks the men to follow him into his bedroom. From the top drawer of his dresser, he extracts an envelope, and from the envelope a thick wad of bills totaling five thousand dollars. This is all he has left from the sale, Timothy explains, and he offers the money to Blackbeard. In return for this gesture of good faith, he asks that Blackbeard be reasonable, and understand two things: first, that you cannot get water from a stone, and second, that a bale of marijuana is not a lost puppy, or an umbrella. When a man finds one, he can't be expected to hold onto it until the rightful owner comes around.

Blackbeard's face darkens, and Timothy adds that he will do everything possible to help the sailor recover his property from the man now in possession.

This man, Timothy assures him, is no stone.

Blackbeard stares at the professor for a moment, eyes narrow in the leathery pockets of his skin. Then he takes the envelope, hands it to his colleague, and growls, "Well?"

Haltingly, as if already regretting the deal, Timothy tells Blackbeard that the buyer is a man of tremendous wealth and discretion, whose name he does not know. But he is staying on a 168-foot yacht called *The Southern Breeze*; it is anchored in the middle of Vineyard Haven Harbor, between the drawbridge and the yacht club, accessible only by small craft. One must give the security guard a password in order to come aboard. The required phrase is "Cigar delivery from Mr. Castro."

Blackbeard departs with threats and invective, pledging to return if Timothy's rich customer gives him any trouble at all. That night, he and his colleague pilot a dinghy out to the yacht, equipped with a password, a plan, and a cache of small arms. They are not heard from again.

A wholly different version of the story holds that the entire bale of marijuana is eaten by goats. This is either accidental, or orchestrated. If orchestrated, the idea is to slaughter the livestock and sell the THC-laden meat, as a low-risk, high-reward method of alchemizing the marijuana into money.

This tale is always set in the mid-1980s, when recreational cocaine use is widespread, and hair-brained schemes abound. Most accounts claim the goats are killed as planned, and that for the remainder of the summer, the menu of a fine-dining establishment in Chilmark (long gone now, but infamous throughout the Reagan years for occasionally paying its kitchen staff in narcotics) features a fifty-eight-dollar braised goat stew. Despite the price, exorbitant even by the standards of Vineyard eateries, the dish sells out consistently.

An alternate telling has the goats, stoned out of their gourds, wandering off their owner's property and laying tragicomic siege to a large outdoor wedding party being held on an adjacent plot. But such a thing is clearly too outrageous to be taken seriously.

PART II

SUMMER PEOPLE

PART II

BAD NIGHT IN HYANNISPORT

BY SETH GREENLAND

Hyannisport

I was dead. That was the main thing. And I never saw it coming. Maybe if I hadn't been suffering from the worst hangover of my life I would have sensed something was amiss. The aftermath of a tequila bender can do that to you—dull your perceptions, make you a tad less sharp, create a membrane between you and reality that will keep your receptors from taking in the subtle signals that often spell the difference between survival and oblivion. That was the extent of the wisdom I had accrued over a lifetime: I was an expert on hangovers. But what do you expect from someone who had just turned nineteen?

This was 1974 and it had already been a strange year. Abba had won the Eurovision Song Contest but back then bad music was the least of it. Everything was crap. Bleak and corrupt. The Watergate saga had unspooled and Nixon had resigned. It was the middle of August and I had just finished my freshman year at a famous university. Here is all I will say about the school: you probably couldn't get in. I don't mean to sound arrogant. People have told me I can come off that way. But is it arrogance if it's the truth? You probably *couldn't* get in. Don't kill the messenger.

I was spending that summer as a construction worker on Cape Cod. We were building condos in Hyannisport, not far from the Kennedy family compound. My job was to build forms, wooden structures into which concrete for the foundations would be poured. I was the only college kid on the crew and I spent my lunch hours sitting alone, eating bologna on white bread, and reading *Atlas Shrugged*. I wasn't being a snob. I could just tell the other guys didn't want to talk to me. Early in the summer I thought I had a friend on the crew, this guy Bob. He was around my age and had a sister. She was a couple of years younger and middling attractive. They were locals. I took her out one night, slipped something in her drink, and made it with her on the beach in Harwichport. I wasn't sure if she remembered when she woke up. A couple of days later, Bob asked if I planned to call her, but I didn't see the point. Although Bob and I were together at work all the time, he didn't speak to me again until he told me she was pregnant. How was that my problem? I asked. Bob said he was going to kick my ass. I told him to try it.

Every night after work, I'd go to the beach. I'd swim out and pull off my shorts and float until the last rays of the sun disappeared over the horizon. As peaceful a scene as you could imagine, like a Winslow Homer painting that hung in the art museum at school. All this naked swimming had one profound effect: it made me incredibly horny. Nineteen-year-old boys are notorious hormonal cauldrons, but there was something about the feel of salt water against naked skin that induced a sensuality so sublime I desperately wanted someone to share it with. I already told you I wasn't interested in Bob's sister. So it was after one of these twilight immersions that I decided to call Margaret Shaughnessy.

Ah, Margaret, light of my life, fire of my loins! Yes, I know Nabokov wrote that in another context—we did him in freshman English—and Margaret was nineteen, not whatever age Dolores Haze was, but you get the idea. We had met two years earlier in Chamonix, France. Please don't think I'm some jet-setting dickweed who casually wings to Europe for coke-and-

champagne-fueled skiing jaunts. It was my first time in France.
I was there with my suburban Connecticut high school ski club
and Margaret was with her family. We met standing in line at
a ski lodge where I was trying to order sausages in my eleventh
grade French. We spent the rest of the day gliding down gla-
ciers cutting S-curves in the snow. That night we got drunk on
Tuborg (no one checks IDs in France) and we skied together
for the rest of the week. A mane of thick, honey-blond hair
cascaded over her shoulders and down to the middle of her
back. The perfection of her white teeth was rendered more
exquisite by virtue of being marred by the left incisor leaning
slightly out of alignment. Her skin, burnished by the Alpine
sun, was flawless, although now would be a good time to say I
never got to lay a hand on it. Our brief European idyll ended
and we both returned to our American hometowns. Her family lived in the Boston area so we found ourselves more than
a hundred miles apart. A few letters were exchanged, then we
promptly lost touch.

Margaret's family had a summer house in Hyannis. She
had not forgotten me and we made plans to go out. Roomful of
Blues were playing at a local club called Connie's and I was no
stranger to the unlikely aphrodisiacal nature of the 1940s-style
swing they purveyed. If Margaret couldn't swing dance I would
teach her how. And then sex would ensue.

Nonunion construction workers didn't make a lot of money
on Cape Cod in 1974 and I had no intention of spending what
little I had on drinks. So before picking Margaret up in my blue
1969 Peugeot, I purchased a pint of tequila. When I knocked
on the door of her family's sprawling house Margaret answered
and looked exactly as I remembered her. The diffidence was
new, but I ascribed that to not having seen each other in two
years. Her parents loomed disapprovingly in the hallway. Gray
and thin-lipped, they were a matching set ordered from an L.L.

Bean catalog. Margaret's mother would develop Alzheimer's. Her father would die from a massive heart attack. I could tell they didn't like me so I shot them my best Burt Reynolds smile and hustled their ripe daughter into the beckoning evening.

On the drive to the club, Margaret told me she had just finished her freshman year at the University of New Hampshire. I had no problem with that. It wasn't like I was going to marry her. I asked her what she planned to major in and, honestly, it's hard for me to remember her answer. She sounded less interested in it than I was. Next came some desultory reminiscing about the few days we had spent together in France. By the time we arrived at the club, I was afraid we might have exhausted the conversational possibilities for the evening.

Connie's had once been a large, private home but walls had been ripped out and a bar and dance floor installed. Now the place jumped from June to Labor Day. I paid the cover charge and we sat at a table and ordered beers as we continued to chat about nothing. Margaret liked college. She was working as a waitress at a clam shack for the summer. One of her brothers had beaten the shit out of a guy she'd been dating and served six months in jail for assault. What? That was interesting. He'd just been released and had moved back in with Margaret's parents. I asked her why he had done it and she told me it was because she had asked him. Did I want to meet him? Not really, I said. Then she laughed like she was kidding about the whole thing.

The band started to play and they were terrific. I had been eager for them to go on because I was hoping that, however difficult our verbal communication was, Margaret and I might find communion on the dance floor. But when I stood in front of her with my hand extended in my best Fred-to-Ginger gesture, she demurred. "I don't know how to dance to this," she said. I told her it didn't matter, that it was easy, that I would teach her. I might as well have been talking to a lobster. The vivacity of the music, revelers popping and jiving all around us, the beers—nothing made an impression. It was then I realized that smoothly moving along a French glacier in a haze of sunshine and Tuborg will make anyone seem fascinating. I sat back down and stared at the band, who were tearing their way through "Choo Choo Ch'boogie" by Louis Jordan. Margaret went to the ladies' room. My plan for the evening was not working and clearly I needed another. I drained the remainder of my second beer, removed the pint of tequila from my pocket and emptied the contents into the beer glass: sixteen ounces of pure Jose Cuervo. Over the next ninety minutes, I proceeded to drink every last drop. I have absolutely no recollection of what I discussed with Margaret. All I remember is that the tequila made the conversation a lot more scintillating than what had come before. But I was tired of not dancing.

I excused myself and stepped out on the small dance floor where I began to do the modified neo-lindy hop that passed for swing dancing in the post-hippie era. This is not the easiest thing to do without a partner. I looked completely spastic but I didn't care what these people thought. Two taps of the left foot, two taps of the right, and I swung my arms around and spun, accidentally slapping the woman next to me hard across the face with the back of my hand. Her boyfriend took exception to this and smashed his fist into my chin, causing me to crash into a table where another couple was sitting. I heard breaking glass and the girl—blond, topsiders, and a tight red Lacoste shirt that encased striving breasts—swore loudly. As I was trying to stand, the bouncer grabbed my elbow. He was a gorilla in a Bruins jersey and when he escorted me outside, I made sure to tell him the Bruins sucked. Maybe that's why he threw me to the pavement and kicked me in the gut.

I was spitting tequila-flavored stomach juice out of my

mouth when I looked up and saw Margaret staring at me as if I were a traffic accident. I asked if she'd like a ride home but she told me she had already called her jailbird brother and he was on his way. This did not sound promising. I had no intention of meeting him so I said I'd call her and lurched toward my car.

Unsure of the way home, I gunned the Peugeot into the night. One turn, then another—in complete control of the car, thank you very much—and I found myself in Hyannisport. Traffic was remarkably light, and all going in the other direction. I was quite pleased with myself. The alcohol coursing through my bloodstream coated the recent events in a patina of hazy amusement, and I ascribed the evening to experience, a story I would tell the three guys from school with whom I was sharing a ramshackle garage apartment. Tomorrow, I surmised— ever the optimist—would be a better day. The flashing red and blue lights in my rearview mirror put a toe tag on that thought. I cursed under my breath and pulled over.

A bright light shone in my eyes. I squinted. "Can I help you, officer?" I asked.

The cop was young, in his twenties. He had pasty white skin and black hair, cut short. As he scoured the interior of the car with his flashlight it occurred to me that I might be more inebriated than I realized. He asked for my license and registration. I handed them to him with the most helpful-seeming alacrity. If I could convey the essential sweet harmlessness of my nature, I knew he would just wave me along.

"You know where you are?"

"Hyannisport."

"This is a one-way street, and you're driving the wrong way," he said, to my immense chagrin. Then he ordered me out of the car where, beside the curb, illuminated by the headlights of the patrol car, I performed the DUI ballet: walk in a straight line one foot directly in front of the other, touch your nose, turn around, and repeat. I executed it perfectly. So I was stunned when he told me to place my hands behind my back.

"Exactly what do you think you're doing?" I asked as he slipped the cuffs on, like I was Mr. Howell and he was Gilligan. He told me I was under arrest, which came as a shock, although in retrospect the handcuffs should have been a giveaway. Then he told me to shut the fuck up. In a Boston accent. Which I hate. The tequila said he should go fuck his mother. I noticed his name tag read, *O'Rourke*. He shoved me in the backseat of his car.

"Do you have any idea who I am?" I asked, as Officer O'Rourke drove toward the police station.

"You're the dipshit I just arrested," he replied.

"I think you're missing my point," I said. "I pay taxes, so that means you work for me. Take me home."

O'Rourke laughed, but it wasn't the kind of laugh you hear when a guy thinks something is funny. It was a little brutal. "Maybe you shouldn't talk."

"I'll do all the talking I want," I said. Yes, I was sitting handcuffed in the backseat of a Hyannisport police car, conversing with this submoron O'Rourke, but he would have to release me eventually and I'd have another piquant detail to add to the saga this evening had become. What would O'Rourke have? Another shitty night, then home to a beer and bad TV. I told him that. What was he going to do? Beat me to death? O'Rourke grunted in reply. Then I threw up in the back of his patrol car. Up came the tequila, along with the cheeseburger and fries I had eaten for dinner. I was careful to cant my body forward and didn't get any on my khakis or white Brooks Brothers polo shirt. I told O'Rourke that if he had let me go he wouldn't be stuck scraping the reeking detritus of my stomach off his backseat. Then I asked him if he knew what the word *detritus* meant. He did not say. Instead, he cursed me volubly. I asked him how he liked his job. More curses flew my way. I laughed at O'Rourke and took pains to let him know I was laughing at him. When I was done laughing, I said: "You fucking loser." Then I said: "Do you *really* not know who I am?" It wasn't like I was really anybody, but I was better than O'Rourke and wanted him to know it. He didn't answer. I got a glimpse of his face in the rearview mirror. He had that look Elmer Fudd gets right before he shoots Bugs Bunny. Then Elmer pulls the trigger and the shotgun blows up in his face. I asked him if he ever watched Bugs Bunny. O'Rourke would be killed in a one-car accident on Route 28 nine years later. If I had known that at the time, I might have treated him better.

When we arrived at the police station, O'Rourke led me into the squad room. There were five officers there and they all looked as if they had just returned from a saturated fat convention. "If this is what the police force looks like," I remarked, making sure it was loud enough for them all to hear, "no wonder crime in America is exploding." It was like talking to a painting, but not a real painting by an actual artist—more like the kind where dogs play poker. I sat down and one of the fat bastards requested I blow into a straw attached to something that looked like an old radio. It was a breathalyzer, someone explained. I was bored with the conversation—honestly, it was like throwing a tennis ball at a marshmallow wall—so I did what they asked. This would be a good time to tell you that I received a nearly perfect score on my college boards. I was accustomed to doing well on tests, so when I registered a 0.27 on the breathalyzer, I wasn't surprised. 0.08 is considered drunk. At the time I found this very amusing, but my laughter failed to move them.

I was allowed a phone call. I couldn't contact my father who was presumably asleep in our house in Connecticut. He was an attorney at a Wall Street firm and this arrest would not comport with his worldview, in which his son progressed seamlessly from high school to college to law school, partnership, marriage, and high-achieving children, without any detours into jail cells along the way. So I called Bob, the guy from my construction crew. We had been friends when the summer began and I thought if I explained the situation, he would let bygones be bygones and bail me out. Bob was surprised to hear from me and I could tell he was about to hang up until I let him know where I was. He said he'd meet me in court the next day. I'm not sure why I called him other than I was smashed and not thinking rationally. I should have been suspicious when he agreed to come.

The cell was about half the size of my dorm room. Unlike my dorm room, it had a steel toilet and a steel bed. It was down a hallway with several other cells, all of them empty. (Apparently, I was a one-man crime wave.) There was a large metal door at the end of the hallway and when the cop who had escorted me to my cell departed it closed with unsettling finality. For about five minutes I sat there and stared into space, angry, humiliated—no, *insulted*—that I was being treated this way. Then I began to yell. I cursed, screamed imprecations, made demands. This went on for a while. My throat became raw. I was beginning to feel dehydrated. The brutes in the next room continued to ignore my cries. Eventually, after it became clear that they couldn't care less whether I lived or died, I lay down on the metal rack and tried to sleep. My mouth tasted like the inside of a sneaker, my eyes were brittle, and my ribs ached from when that ape at the nightclub kicked me. I thought about what it would be like to spend the rest of my life in a cell. I decided I'd rather be dead. Was this where they'd taken Margaret's brother after he beat up her ex-boyfriend? Was that story even true? And if it was, it occurred to me he might know some of these cops. Would they let him into the cells to work me over with a truncheon? But I hadn't really done anything to Margaret other than embarrass her, so maybe I was safe.

Somehow, a facsimile of sleep arrived, and when I awakened it felt as if a flock of tiny raptors were battling in my skull, their spiny wings throbbing against my delicate membranes. Pain like I had never known radiated down the left side of my head and to my neck. It sang in unbridled cacophony to my quivering tendons and hollow bones. As soon as I realized where I was, the feeling intensified. I was too dehydrated to urinate so I sat frozen in a vortex of self-pity until I heard the metal door open. Was this someone coming to exact revenge, to beat me in all the places that would never show when I stood in court? No, just a cop unlocking the cell door. He said he was taking me to be arraigned.

In the courtroom, I looked for Bob, but he was nowhere to be seen. Maybe he'd had no real intention of showing up, his little revenge. The judge was a bald man with black horn-rims who asked me how I pled. "Not guilty," I responded. My plan: take the money I had made that summer, hire a lawyer, and have this stain removed. *Out, damned spot*, right? My father would never have to know and my future legal career would go as planned.

I was given a court date and released on my own recognizance. I didn't need Bob to post bail after all. When I left the building, sunlight eviscerated my eyes. The tiny raptors continued to beat against the inside of my skull. Bile sluiced through my gut as I wobbled down the courthouse steps. I heard someone calling my name. It was Bob. He was backlit by the sun so it was hard to see the expression on his face, but I could tell the person standing next to him was his sister. Was she going to shoot me or do something equally trite? Bob said she wanted to have a word and I had better do her the courtesy of listening, but I was in no condition for a sidewalk colloquy with a one-night stand and I said as much. I didn't see Bob's fist, but the blood pouring out of my face an instant later suggested he had broken my nose. The pain, of course, penetrated the penumbra of my hangover and I felt like a grenade had discharged in my sinuses. The blood-soaked white polo shirt looked like a crime scene as I staggered away, the pathetic maledictions of Bob's sister raining down on me. Why are people so unbelievably annoying?

The Peugeot had been taken to the police garage so I walked the short way there from the courthouse. The guy in charge of the motor pool, prematurely gray with hawkish features and a scar on his left cheek, stared at me and didn't say anything. I looked down at my bloody shirt and shrugged. "A bad night in Hyannisport," I said. He nodded warily and told me there was a problem with the transmission. If I wanted, he would fix it, but it wouldn't be ready until the afternoon. The oil stink of the garage was making me nauseous and I had to get out of there. I thanked the man and told him I'd be back later. Then I thanked him again. I remembered enough of the previous night to recall that after my arrest my behavior had left something to be desired, and today I was going to make up for it. I'm not a bad guy. I thanked him a third time before I left.

The walk home from Hyannisport to West Dennis was about ten miles. My hangover seemed to have gained in intensity and I thought a cocktail of fresh air and sunshine might make it dissipate. The list of places more beautiful than Cape Cod in August is a short one. As the salt breeze filled my nostrils, I noticed that a few dabs of ochre and yellow had begun to peek through the leaves. I headed east along the blacktop, still trying to will my hangover into submission and humming the opening of "Immigrant Song" by Led Zeppelin. Their drummer, the great John Bonham, would be dead from drink six years later. The temperature was in the nineties by now and I was beginning to perspire. By the time I hummed my way through the song once, I knew I didn't want to walk.

I stuck my thumb out and two cars passed me, a Volvo station wagon and a Ford Pinto. Wouldn't it be just my luck, I reflected, if Margaret and her brother drove past? Was she kidding when she told me he had been in jail for beating up her old boyfriend? I still couldn't figure that one out. Sometimes people said things just to play with your head. And what if Bob and his sister happened by? It wasn't like I could run. A red Malibu with mag wheels pulled to a stop. I approached and looked in through the rolled-down passenger window at Officer O'Rourke. This was a stroke of luck. It's not often the possibility of redemption presents itself in so convenient a way.

"I'm really sorry about last night," I said. "I acted like an idiot."

"Where you headed?" His face was neutral, but cops are like that. I said I was going to West Dennis and he told me he could take me most of the way. I got in the front seat. O'Rourke was dressed in civilian clothes: painter's pants and a gray T-shirt that said, *Eddie's Seafood Shack, Since 1972.* That was a joke, since it was 1974. Eddie obviously had a good sense of humor, which was more than I could say for O'Rourke. There was a snub-nosed revolver on his hip. We rode in silence for a minute. This made me uncomfortable. I like small talk.

"How long you been a cop?" I asked, leaving out the word *have* in an attempt to be familiar.

"Five years."

I nodded. It was clear O'Rourke wasn't interested in talking. I settled into the seat. At my feet there were a pile of eight track tapes: Blue Oyster Cult, Deep Purple, Bachman Turner Overdrive. Utter crap. I hated all of it but wanted to be friendly.

"Okay if we listen to some music?"

"Sure," he said, as he picked up the BTO tape and slid it into the player. "You Ain't Seen Nothing Yet" filled the car. I closed my eyes and sighed. Wouldn't it be ridiculous, I thought, if this shit was the last thing I ever heard?

SPECTACLE POND

BY LIZZIE SKURNICK

Wellfleet

Albert was going to clean out the house. This had been decided weeks ago by his aging aunt June, although if you asked Albert, which it was unlikely anyone would, the circumstances that sent him—not his older brother Mark, or even Mark's nineteen-year-old only daughter Ludi, whereabouts undetermined—from Queens to Cape Cod had been set in motion decades before, perhaps by his and Mark's dead parents, or even, Albert suspected, when Aunt June's husband Travis first bought the house as an investment property, then decamped immediately for parts unknown.

As June rattlingly related to Albert from Horizon Wind, her active seniors community in Charlotte, North Carolina, in the last three years his older brother had joined an actor's collective in the Appalachians—although on more precise details she was spotty. In the wake of his wife Susan's tragic death, Albert had made a habit of calling June every two weeks. When she moved to Horizon Wind, he drove down to Charlotte to help carry the few treasured possessions—June was not one to treasure—from her ten-room Larchmont Georgian. Then June rebuffed his offer of one last nice dinner out. Surrounded by new social possibilities, like a gawky teenager in a college dorm, his seventy-three-year-old aunt was vaguely mortified, he realized, by his presence.

Ludi's coordinates were less certain. After the accident that killed Albert's wife, she returned to her mother; how often Mark had visited the girl during this period Albert did not know. He himself descended into a stinking waste of bourbon for a few years, abetted by a job that required little more effort than showing up. No one was riding a telemarketing firm's accountant. Yet it was partly his money that, years later, allowed Ludi to debark from her small liberal arts school in New Hampshire to communicate, Albert understood from June, primarily with her father only by the occasional phone call or e-mail from abroad. June too claimed she was the recipient of a stray postcard from Barcelona or Kharkov, although Albert was dubious. But despite the improbability of the situation, despite the fact that the girl throughout her life had been removed from their family's orbit for jarring and indeterminate periods of time, June had always claimed Ludi as her own.

The house ex-Uncle Travis purchased on Chequessett Neck Road in Wellfleet was not beachfront property. Set back in scrubby pines, it was enclosed in near twenty-four-hour darkness that Albert, clutching a small overnight bag and a paper tray of clam strips he'd purchased on Route 6, was relieved he could find.

The patch of bare needles they called the driveway was a ringing, chill silence. During the summer, that road had enclosed them in sleepy, chattering darkness, like voices from a party in another room. In late October, the air was a wall built to expel intruders. He approached the screen door, hoping, though the catch had been broken for at least twenty years, he might find it locked.

Travis bought the house before Mark and Albert's parents died in a train accident. June handled this well. The boys were fourteen and fifteen, she reasoned, not five. Albert remembered standing by the grave after the funeral, feeling that he should ape June's matter-of-fact behavior, click-clacking in mourning black out the door to the funeral home. She'd arranged a double ceremony with black coffins Mark said looked like cannons. Albert heartily shook everyone's hand until June took him aside and placed him on a chair near the door.

Inside the house, Albert put his bag down and flipped on the lights. The sepia floral sconces seemed defeated by the redwood walls. Even from across the room, Albert could see the skinlike layer of dust covering the green couch. June had seemed confident that he could simply remove her personal items, give the house a scrubbing, and hand the keys over to a realtor, who would sell the place for enough money to keep her at Horizon Wind for another twenty years.

Albert didn't doubt the house would sell, but he understood now that a simple cleaning would not suffice. During his bourbon months, he had seen "staging" makeovers on home improvement shows. This place was in such disorder it would be faster to empty it, have it professionally cleaned, and let the buyers, who would certainly knock it down and build one of the new sandboxes lining the road anyway, have it for cheap. June wouldn't like it, but she would have no choice. "You have to forgive, Albert," she had said when Susan died. "We're family, and you have to forgive." Now, June would have to forgive too.

Albert remembered the loop of summers. First, the beach at Newcomb Hollow, then Long Pond or Great Pond, followed by sandwiches from the Box Lunch, and lobsters—when June allowed—grilled by the porch. He and Mark would run on the bay side, by the house, where they once, at low tide, tried to swim across to Indian Neck Beach. June shouted until they gave up halfway, returning in slimy bay silt.

Rainy days, they went to Provincetown. This, in the 1970s, was truly the land of the "boys." Mark stared openly.

Albert was ashamed—not for himself, but for the men, whom he obscurely felt needed his reassurance. Later, in college, he realized his reassurance was not needed in this or any other areas. June had started to rent the house during the high season and go to Boca. Mark began a series of wanderings from California to India to South America, which even Albert knew enough to dismiss as the check-off destinations of their generation.

When he was in his early twenties, the family began spending Augusts at the house again. Albert married Susan. But Mark had a child. Aunt June liked Susan, yet seemed faintly astonished that Albert had a managed to get a wife at all, as if he'd suddenly revealed a secret mastery of the grand piano, or invented the Post-it. Mark was friendly to Susan, but when was he not? He was so friendly that he had brought home girl-friend after girlfriend from the time Albert was seventeen, culminating, around the time of Albert's marriage, with a black woman named April.

April was a tall and somewhat forbidding professor of English. Always a little distant, always a bit apart. Albert could never tell whether this had to do with character, intellect, or was simply a defensive reaction to his strange family. There was June, a distracted, wizened chain smoker; the birdlike, chattering Susan, incapable of not flirting with Mark, whose appeal to all women Albert had long since accepted. Albert had difficulty gauging his own presence. He would have liked to think of himself as a comforting figure, calm and self-contained, but in her two Thanksgivings and one Easter with the family, April had barely said two words to him. She had a son from an earlier marriage whom they never met, and shortly after giving birth to Ludi, she kicked Mark out, only releasing the girl at Mark's insistence after a year.

Given free rein, June revealed a maternal nature that had

heretofore found no avenue for expression. Ludi, at age two, had a face like a beautiful smudge, almost a thumbprint of itself, and June delighted in pulling her black silken hair, which April had delivered braided, into soft pigtails that helped frame her gap-toothed grin. Those summer years, in Albert's memory, seemed almost a constant series in partial visibility: Ludi in profile, bent over with a book in June's lap, or departing, held aloft in June's arms, head on the middle-aged woman's shoulder.

Once, when April was living in New York and Mark was held up somewhere on unspecified "business," Albert and Susan picked up the girl to drive her to the Cape. Albert was shocked at her surroundings. He'd pictured April in a bohemian but charming area, someplace in the city that would be new for him and Susan, different from their three-bedroom in Forest Hills. Instead, deep in Brooklyn, it was the kind of neighborhood where playgrounds were made of steel piping and concrete, as if to emphasize their durability. There was charmless green paint over all the streetlights.

"I have her bathing suit in her bag," April said pointedly. Last year, it had been nowhere to be found, a brief matter of contention when Ludi was returned with a pink flowered bikini Mark had picked up in a roadside shop.

"She'll have a wonderful time," Albert said, grasping the girl's hand. Ludi seemed to know him, looking up with a smile. He was shocked to find himself rocked with a wave of protective affection. He squeezed her hand and Ludi forgot immediately who he was. She ran to the car, where Susan opened the door to welcome her with outstretched arms, then waved to April.

"She'll have a wonderful time," he said to April again, who was looking at him skeptically. She had aged very little but looked far less happy—unsurprising, Albert thought, if she had been brought low enough to live in this place. Mark's bootless wandering certainly couldn't have been contributing to the household. Albert thought again how stupid a name Ludi had been to give to the girl, a play on Liudmila, a favorite character of April's from some Russian novel. It was one of the many crimes his absentee brother had helped visit upon his daughter.

"I'm sure she will," April said, making to close the door, then paused. "Tell Mark I say hello," she added carefully. It was always hard to grasp the essence of any couple, but for Albert, April and Mark were harder than most.

In the morning, Albert awoke and immediately felt glad of the silence and the lack of tourist traffic, which would make it easier for him to get the furniture hauled away and clean the house. He fished out one of June's phone books from under the filigreed, fake wood counter. It was ten years out-of-date.

He decided to walk into Wellfleet. The Bookstore Restaurant, where he and Mark had once fingered stacks of overpriced vintage comics, was closed for the weekend, as was the small ice cream and candy stand at the end of the dock. Galleries had begun to spring up on Water Street toward the center of town, but Albert was not moved to examine them. It was the kind of thing Susan had liked.

The summer she died, she had taken to making flowery observations about the region, hauling out maps to show a now-gawky Ludi that the ponds—Great Pond, Gull Pond, Long Pond, Spectacle Pond—looked like fingers, as if God had pressed His hand into the damp ground and let the impression fill with mud, then water.

Albert had wondered whether Susan thought of these things in advance to announce to the girl, or if they sprung from her on the spot. Toward the end, it seemed a kind of mania, to be so lyrical about everything. *Put it in a poem*, he felt like saying. Once he *had* actually said it. Ludi and Susan had spent the weekend writing just such poems, and when Mark returned Sunday from wherever he had gone, he had them framed. This was exactly the type of item, Albert assumed, June wanted removed before he handed over the keys to Chequessett Realty.

Susan's death was an accident. Albert was told this, in the moment, so frequently, with such calm assurance, by so many faceless authorities, that it was only when he had roused himself from grief, and then paralysis, that he found to his surprise he could nominally agree.

Mark had not been drunk, or returning late from one of his trips, or any of the many things it would have been easier to blame him for. He was picking up Ludi from the parking lot of the Great Island Walk. She was allowed to take the hike partway alone, now that she was fourteen.

Albert and Susan had gone on this very walk with Ludi many times, although they seldom made it to the end of the three hunchbacked mounds that stretched out to the ocean. Ludi liked to haul herself over to the oceanside a mile in and pick through rocks, even when she was old enough, Albert felt, to be beyond such things. At least she had stopped examining hermit crabs. It was not uncommon for Susan and Ludi to gather a pound of unvariegated shards and give them to Albert to carry up the dirt-cut stairs when they were done.

That summer, relations between Susan and Ludi seemed strained. Albert had chalked it up to Ludi's adolescence. He noticed it particularly on a trip to Provincetown the weekend before the accident. Instead of raiding jewelry shops with Susan, Ludi stuck close to Albert. He would have thought she'd take interest in the drag queens who had begun to pop up in abundance, but instead she was fascinated by the lesbian couples, especially the biracial ones.

"Why do you think so many of the girl couples are black and white?" she asked Albert when Susan, after many unsuccessful attempts at conversation, darted off to find a bathroom.

It may have been the first serious question Ludi had ever asked him, and he was surprised to find himself with an answer. "I guess after you cross one boundary, it doesn't matter if you cross another one," he said.

Had this hurt the girl's feelings? It was only later that night that Albert remembered Ludi herself was biracial, something he knew, of course, but had failed to associate with the girl. At fourteen, how sensitive would Ludi have been?

Susan returned from the bathroom and linked her arm with Ludi's. "There are all kinds of families," she told them. "All kinds of different constellations."

Albert hadn't known she was listening. Maybe she was referring to their own childless state. That summer, their lovemaking also bloomed into a kind of mania, Susan frantically assuming new positions, climaxing so loudly he'd shushed her once or twice, afraid she would wake up June or the girl. Was she, at thirty-seven, desperate to have a baby, or had she abandoned the idea, and was trying to make do with what was left?

"You just like to come," she accused him. It wasn't untrue. He couldn't decide a position on children either, and was happy for Susan to lead the way. Then, around the time of the trip to Provincetown, Susan relaxed, a catlike smile spreading across her features. It was in this mood that she approached Albert and Ludi, and it was probably the same mood in which, not long after, she ran out to greet Mark and Ludi as they pulled into the parking space.

In the slight wood surrounding the house on Chequessett

Neck Road, around four o'clock every day, a sharp needle of light appeared as the sun set over the bay, sliding to midpoint on one of the larger trees until it was eaten by the dusk. It was this needle that hit Mark directly in the eye and blinded him as he pulled in with the car. Three hours later, Susan was dead, and another twelve hours after that, the coroner told Albert that his wife had been seven weeks pregnant.

Albert was weeping. He wasn't sure why he'd thought gathering the paltry leavings of his scattered family wouldn't set him off, but it had been a long time since he'd cried for Susan, or any of them.

There was a picture of Ludi's graduation. The sight of the girl—now tall, almost obscenely comely, with ripe lips and languid, sleepy eyes—made Albert draw back with physical distaste. Since Susan's death, he hadn't seen her. Ludi looked both like Mark and like her mother, who had elected to attend the ceremony in a different portion of the seating and take Ludi for a dinner with her friends the night before.

He placed June's few wall hangings and prints in a box, then pulled a stack of photo albums off the bottom of a bookshelf filled with paperbacks he would not bother to save.

He knew what was in the albums. On rainy days, when they were teenagers, he and Mark would look at pictures of their parents: his mother's high school graduation photo, with the black velvet sweetheart neckline over her shoulders; the wedding photo; some early shots of the family on the lawn of their house in Edison, New Jersey; his baby picture and Mark's. At some point, June had added a series of Ludi to the album, and Albert was shocked to see how much she resembled his own mother also, of whom he rarely thought. How strange not to remember one's childhood. But Albert was beginning to feel that, in his case, it was more a matter of failing to pay attention. His life—his attentiveness—seemed to have begun only at his parents' death, and culminated with Susan's. Perhaps that's why Aunt June had backed away from him, and Mark, who had maintained a decent tether throughout their twenties and thirties, absented himself completely. Perhaps Albert's lack of attention was prescriptive.

He was cramming a stack of maps into a garbage bag when he realized they were the ones Susan and Ludi had used to write those poems so long ago. He took the sheaf of poems, now removed from their frames, and placed them carefully in a neat stack. There were odes to Long Pond, Great Pond, even Indian Neck Road, some in Ludi's careful, halting hand, and the rest in Susan's confident, round script. Spectacle Pond: *You can barely see the forest for the trees.* That was Ludi. *This road leads only one way, but the sand leads two.* Vintage Susan. Where else would the sand be but on two sides, on the Cape?

He turned the poem over.

All my love, Your Susan, it said.

Susan was the one who had wanted to go to Spectacle Pond. "It's the only one we haven't seen," she'd said.

Albert knew Spectacle Pond. It was barely good for swimming, just two flat rounds of shallow water off Long Pond Road. He had been there once as a teenager with Mark, who found it beautiful. Albert preferred Great Pond, which by that age he had mastered swimming across.

The road to Spectacle Pond was not paved. It was deep, hardened mud, and several times Albert had to back the car up to keep the tires in the grooves. "I hope you like it," he said. There was no answer, and for a moment he felt certain that Susan was restraining herself from telling him to shut up.

At the pond, there was no proper beach, only the same gaping mud, stringy with reeds. "Come in, darling," Susan said to Ludi. "It's creepy," the girl replied. Finally, she joined Susan in the center, where Susan held her, as if she were still two years old. "Look up!" Susan urged, pointing at the enclosed circle of sky. "Isn't it beautiful? From above, it looks like eyes!" On the shore, Albert heard Ludi either snort or murmur something like agreement.

Ludi had refused to step in the other pond. "It's exactly the same!" Susan exclaimed. "That's what I mean," Ludi said, her voice filled with that quiet Albert had only begun to learn, in children, meant terror. "Go wait in the car," Susan said, suddenly impatient. "I'm going to go under, and so are you, Albert."

How angry had he been as he waded out into the water and dunked his head? He couldn't remember. He only knew that when they returned to the car, Ludi's face floated out at them, ghostly, accusatory. She was in his seat. "Don't be afraid," he said.

All my love, Your Susan. On the back of the poem that Mark had had framed. He looked at that a long time.

But Ludi hadn't answered that she wasn't afraid. She had said: "I can drive."

He could see them, even now, as he walked by the bay, hovering over his wife, June emerging from the house, cigarette in hand. Was there any chance she hadn't known? It seemed unlikely. She would have colluded immediately, as would Ludi, who, after all, would only be continuing in her mode of silent and opaque adolescence. By the time Susan was in the morgue and her death dispatched as accidental manslaughter, Mark had disappeared with the girl. June had, with relief, seen her younger nephew off. Now he understood.

Now he understood a lot of things, all the signals that he'd missed. Such as Uncle Travis's departure, for instance, which had coincided with the arrival of two teenage boys, or Mark's abiding distance, which seemed less a rejection of his younger brother than a rejection of their relations at the core. They had known—they had all known—and not only had they not protected Albert from their knowledge, he had barely figured in their calculations. Even Susan, no blood relation, still carried more weight in his family than he.

It was dark. He left the house. He was in Spectacle Pond, staring at the water, in the far pond, where Susan and Ludi had looked at the sky. His stomach rose before him like a white moon.

No. There was the actual moon, a delicate, high-set orb, stars twinkling all around it like the crystal earrings Susan often picked off the black velvet trays of vendors in Provincetown. His own stomach was a slab of green cheese, buoyant, like the half-eaten Styrofoam below a float.

He was surprised to find that he was crying again, tears running down his face in hot straight paths. When Susan died, he had cried for years, it seemed—for the first months, vast bellowing gasps of bewilderment, and then a stretch of shamed whimpering that emerged while he was waiting in line at the grocery store or standing in an elevator.

These tears were different—less bewildered and more astonished, as if he had suddenly learned he was adopted, or born on a distant planet. As if *this* world was the distant planet. This was, he supposed, the moment when he was meant to give up, to leave his corpse, his white bloated body, washed up on the needled shore. Or maybe he could seek out Mark, and gun him down in the middle of a performance of *Our Town*. Then he would track down Ludi in whatever hovel she was in, remind her of the many dinners Susan had cooked on her behalf. For a moment, he saw himself dragging her into a cab, shouting orders as some Spanish boyfriend gesticulated in the distance. Albert had never been to Spain.

He was not going to do any of these things. The black sky over the pond was a lid, he suspended in its jar. Through a conflagration of circumstance and other people's will, he was floating alone two miles from a dark small road smack in the center of a barely peopled peninsula, with nobody to know or care. He was not angry or murderous. He was lonely, merely lonely—or at least, he thought, lonelier than anyone like him had right or reason to be.

LA JETÉE

BY DAVID L. ULIN
Harwichport

He had been here before. Countless times before, not the physical space but the emotional space, the roiling space inside. That summer on the Cape, summer he'd turned thirteen, he'd had this . . . *vision* was the only word for it, as if it were a movie in his head. Ever since, it had dogged him, like a distant memory: black-and-white, herky-jerky, somewhere between a film and a collage of stills. Always, he was at the center, moving heedlessly along the jetty, around its great stone curve. He was running from something but he didn't know what, only that it kept coming, relentless, unforgiving, like a simple twist of fate. The jetty made no sense, it was a dead end, a blind alley, but it was where the vision took him, while the big waves crashed against the rocks. He had been drawn here in reality also, drawn to the vastness, to the brackish sweep of steam-drilled boulders, to the tension between industry and nature, the breakwater holding the waves from the harbor and the waves pushing to take it back. They were inevitable, the waves, as inevitable as the vision, in which it was always high tide, and as he tore out past the breakers, the rough water pulled at his feet, until, just beyond the halfway point along the jetty, a big wave crashed across the rocks and swept him out to sea.

Out to sea . . . and didn't that describe him, didn't that get right to where he was? Thirty-eight years old, adrift in a life that didn't fit him any longer, if indeed it ever had. He'd felt it for a long time, the looping tendrils of dissatisfaction, the sharp pangs of regret. Regret for what? He didn't know but recognized the longing, the way that, even in the calmest moments, there was an undertone of discontent.

Now, however, he was really in it; now, it was more than dismay. Over the past few months, his life had narrowed to a pinprick, as if he were being pushed through a series of checkpoints, each one stripping away another piece of who he was. If he'd been a philosopher, he might have seen this as some kind of purification ritual, but he wasn't a philosopher. He was a man.

Or not even a man, not really; not a very good man, anyway. As a kid, he'd sworn that when he grew up, he would pay attention, and here he was living in the fallout of his *in*attention, a junk bond trader in a collapsing market, laid off and understanding in a whole new way what was meant by *out of luck*. The day they'd canned him, he had seen the old man in the corridor, but that fucker hadn't said a word. Instead, he'd disappeared behind the mahogany door of his office—to make lunch plans, to cash out an option, to do God knows what while the HR robots did the dirty work. All morning, people had been summoned, an e-mail or a tap on the shoulder, and then the long walk to the conference room. When his time came, he felt his throat grow dry and a blade of panic slide down his windpipe. He sat for a moment, looking at his computer. There were numbers tracking stock transactions, but as usual they didn't add up. Briefly, he wondered if he should do something—throw the monitor on the floor, hurl his desk chair through a window. Then he got up and trudged down the hall, reminding himself to keep his head up, reminding himself not to let it show.

That was the idea, not to let anyone know it mattered, not to make a scene. In the conference room, they offered water because you couldn't cry when you were drinking water—or at least that's what he'd once heard. *It's not personal*, the robots were saying, *your position has been eliminated*, but it sounded like they were submerged. They handed him a folder with some papers to sign and instructions on how to get his severance, and just like that, he no longer had a job.

He couldn't say how quickly the plan had started to develop, but the earliest inkling came before he'd finished cleaning out his desk. Standing on the jetty, watching the sky grow pale and silver-pink at sunset, he drifted back to that moment, emptying his drawers into a trash can, realizing that nothing he'd gathered in the last five years, nothing he'd accumulated, meant anything at all. In a weird way, he felt hardened, kiln-fired, as if those few minutes in the conference room had heat-blasted him into some new shape. Not purified, though, never purified. Not unless purity could be defined in terms of rage. He'd kept going through his papers, not registering their contents, seeing all those columns of numbers, those transactions, break down into abstract lines. His eyes kept drifting to the old man's office, and he began to imagine what it would be like to walk through that heavy door and slam him through a wall. That little troll—he'd mismanaged the investments, he had overextended, selling short and buying long. Now, all of them had to pay for the mess while the old man went about his business, buying fancy suits and spending weekends on Cape Cod.

But here *he* was on Cape Cod, having taken the Plymouth & Brockton bus from Boston to Hyannis, and the RTA to Harwichport. It was the Monday before Thanksgiving, and he'd come down here for his own kind of celebration, a personal reckoning, Thanksgiving with a kick. He knew this town only from that one long-ago summer and the presence of the jetty in his dreams. But the more he'd thought about it—thought about it? Obsessed about it, sitting in his Central Square apart-

ment in the months since he'd been laid off, watching his severance dwindle down to zero—the more he'd had that sense
of being whittled, of his life leading toward a single moment.
That moment had arrived.

It had been twenty-five years since he'd last been here, and
yet, he knew, there was nowhere else to go. The town hadn't
changed much: the old movie theater was gone, reconfigured
as a shopping complex, with some seasonal stores and a failing
bookshop, and the bakery had moved to a new location, but
otherwise, it was as if he were tracing a passage inside himself.
Unencumbered but for a small backpack, he had wandered
down Main Street, sand rustling in the gutters, sidewalks empty,
summer businesses closed up tight. Past the liquor store and
George's Pizza, through the intersection of Route 28 and Bank
Street, to the residential lanes that led to the bluff. The house
sat on one of these near the end of the blacktop, where the
road dead-ended into an ocean path.

What was it about that summer that had stamped him?
It wasn't like they'd ever belonged. As his father had tried to
play buddy-buddy at the yacht club, he'd ridden his bike, day
after day, alone, adrift, down the summer roads and pathways,
inhaling the silence and feeling it take root in his lungs. Later
that year, the bottom had dropped out on the family, and that,
as they say, was that. Standing here today, though, looking at
the weather-beaten shingles of the house, its eaves and dormer
windows, he'd felt as if time had stopped. Briefly, he thought
about checking it out, but he wasn't ready; instead, he'd followed the narrow trail down the bluff. At the bottom, he stumbled through the dunes, ankle-deep in icy sand, until, after a
hundred yards, he'd come out of the beach grass to see the
flat green tumult of the Atlantic, and off to his left, the jetty
stretching like a question mark across the water beneath the
thin New England autumn light.

That had been an hour ago, and he'd been on the jetty ever since. If he could have found the language, he would have said that he was waiting for the failing of the light. Although the tide was low, the wind was high, and it blew a bitter spray into his eyes. He touched his cheeks. They were wet, salty, as if awash in tears. He wiped the water away, hiked up the back-pack, and buried his hands in the pockets of his pants. Seeing the sky drain of color felt like watching the universe fade out, and the thought brought back the memory of his vision, leaving him to wonder if there was a message in it, a warning sign of things to come.

He waited until the night had wrung the last drops of light out of the sky, until the sand shone silver beneath an early smattering of stars. He waited until he was cold enough to feel as if the stillness of his body and the stillness of the rocks had frozen into one. He waited until the tide began to rise again, the water a series of slow caesuras lapping at the jetty in icy tongues. Then he went back down the beach to the pathway, and up the bluff to the house. For the first time, he allowed himself to take it in. From the outside, it didn't appear any different, a classic Cape Codder, gray clapboard with light blue shutters, same as it had always been.

As a kid that summer, he'd discovered all sorts of things about this rental house: the hidden room above the garage, with its stacks of derelict oil and watercolor paintings; the dusty corners of the basement, where old, overstuffed furniture from the 1940s sat neglected and unkempt. He'd spent days at a time climbing on the outside of the house, pulling himself atop the woodshed, then jumping to the kitchen roof and scrambling to the second floor, where he would crawl around to the upstairs bathroom window, and through it, slip in and out of the house like a ghost. Like a ghost, yes, and if he squinted now, he could almost see himself, transparent as an afterimage, smaller, lighter, not this heavy husk of a man so plodding on his feet. Another piece of himself lost, another incarnation. He shook his head, as if to loosen the web of memory, and came down the driveway, gravel crunching under his shoes.

In the silence, the noise was sharp as gunshots, but the nearby houses were dark and no one was around. He paused for a moment, but this was what he'd been expecting, a community out of season, from the moment the plan began to gel. Back in Cambridge, he had gone on the realty company's website, stared at photos of the house. It had looked the same inside also, iron beds in the bedrooms, the living room with its long couch and two wingchairs, and those shelves of ancient leather books. That was the appeal of it, his father had liked to say, that nothing ever changed on the Cape. It had been the same since the 1950s, the 1940s, the 1920s, those houses with their push-button light switches and mildew from the salt air, those social hierarchies. That summer, he'd thought of this as more of his father's bullshit, when he'd stopped to think of it at all. But gazing at the website, he'd understood that, in this at least, his father was right, and what was more, that it would be of use to him, if he had the nerve to do what needed to be done.

He moved lightly to the end of the driveway, and into the side yard to the back of the house. A canopy of trees stretched out its bare limbs in supplication to the sky. Here, a screened-in porch led to the living room. One more time, he glanced over his shoulder—*nothing, no one*—then put his weight to the screen door and broke the fisheye latch. On the porch, he was hit with an almost physical flood of memory, as if a wave had broken over him. He could see more ghosts: the whisper of his father, drink in hand, sitting in the corner, trying to impress some local blueblood; his mother moving in and out of focus, hands fluttering like little birds. He wondered if these images were real, if they resided in this place, if the house were a repository for every moment, every interaction it had ever contained. He didn't know, hadn't considered that memory would be an issue. Or perhaps it was just that he hadn't wanted to think about that.

He knelt beside the glass door to the living room. It was locked, as he had known it would be. Reaching into the backpack, he withdrew a pair of leather gloves and put them on. Then quickly, savagely, he drove his fist through the pane closest to the handle; it exploded into brilliant shards. The noise reverberated like a bomb blast, and he froze for a moment, before pulling his hand away, glove dotted with small, sparkling stars. Breathing evenly, he let the silence of the evening fall back into place. No ghosts now, no memories, no anything but the feeling that, in punching through the window, he had blown a hole through his own history.

What he was here for, after all, was not nostalgia but the opposite of nostalgia, the end of memory. He had a plan, and it didn't have anything to do with what he'd experienced, or who he once had been. He'd chosen the house because he knew it, and because it was near to where he needed to be. It helped that he had spent so little time here, a single summer, so long ago that it would be difficult to trace any connection to him. *What about that?* he found himself thinking. *How do you like your Cape Cod dream now?* It took a moment to realize that he was addressing his father, that just because he couldn't see them didn't mean the ghosts were gone.

He reached through the broken pane and turned the deadbolt, took hold of the handle, and opened the door. Once inside, he locked the door behind him out of habit, before moving further into the house. In the darkness, he cracked his shin against a small end table but stopped himself before he could cry out. As he rubbed his leg, he let his eyes adjust, making out shapes in the gray blankness of the room. He couldn't see much, just a few spare spectral outlines. The air smelled stale, like furniture that had been shuttered for too long.

Now that he was here, he didn't know where to start. It had seemed so simple back in Cambridge, thinking about the possibilities, watching them narrow down to one. All the pieces were in place: a deserted house in an empty summer town, the confluence of the Thanksgiving holiday, the idea that he would get in and out fast, like an avenging angel, *vengeance is mine saith the Lord*. He didn't believe in that biblical crap, but he was more than happy to be the instrument, to keep the focus, to stand up, in one elusive gesture, for what was right. He had done some other research back in Cambridge, MapQuesting the old man's house in Chatham, figuring out the routes. There wasn't much he could do right now, but somehow he hadn't planned on all this gaping silence, stretching into the darkness like an endless night. *Typical*, he heard a voice say, and for a moment he startled, unsure if it was real. *Never prepared, never paying attention*, and now he could recognize the intonations, the slight slurring of the consonants, the disdain just barely held at bay. Fuck, he thought, as the ghosts descended on the living room, and he could see—*really see*—his father's form take shape by the window, in the wing chair he had favored that summer, sipping gin and tonic, dressed in khakis and Izod, trying to look like he belonged. *You never were much good on the details*, the voice went on, a voice like smoke, coming from nowhere and everywhere, flickering like bad reception but relentless as it had ever been.

It had been a trainwreck, that summer. Of course it had. The rental had been too expensive, and his parents had fought about it every day. His father had seen it as a way to something, but to his mother this had been an empty faith. His father drank too much, and was too loud, too familiar; you could see the others wince as he closed in. And so, he had turned his frustrations first on his wife and then on his son, a scrawny kid then, *the human fly*, his father called him when he saw him scaling the exterior of the house. *What are you doing?* he would yell. *Why can't you be normal for once in your life?* Everything had come to a head one afternoon, when his father had returned to the house to drag him to some useless function and found him hiding in the closet of his room upstairs, curled into a hopeless ball.

It had been years since he'd thought about this, but being in the house brought the memory back in a rush. He could see himself in the corner of the closet, listening as his father's footsteps neared but lacking the will to move. He could see the closet door pull open, feel the violence of it, and see his father's face, flushed with anger, eyes darting as if afraid he would get caught. *Goddamn closet case*, the old man had slobbered, staring down at him. Then he had slammed the door and rushed heavily from the house.

Years later, when his father was dying, he'd mentioned the memory to see what he would say. He didn't know why—to settle the score perhaps, or maybe he just wanted some vindication, an acknowledgment of how it had been.

That never happened, his father had whispered. *I don't know what you're talking about.* But ghosts didn't lie. Or did they? One way or another, he was going to find out.

In the morning, he awoke from uneasy dreams on the living room couch. His back was stiff and his head hurt as if he'd been drinking. For a moment, he couldn't place himself, the angles unfamiliar, light bleeding through the windows in a pale yellow wash. Slowly, awareness crept in: the house, the vision, the jetty, the intercession of all those ghosts.

He sat up, rubbed his eyes. The room was empty, as far as he could see. In the thin November blankness, there was nothing, no whisper of the past. That was good because today he was going to need to be present, he was going to need to pay attention, no matter what his father might have thought.

He pissed for a long time in the downstairs toilet, but the water was turned off so he couldn't flush. No matter, he thought. He wasn't going to be here that long. In the kitchen, he found a box of Cheerios and ate a handful even though they were stale. That summer, he had spent every morning in this kitchen, staring down the endless emptiness of the days that loomed ahead of him like open questions, his only goal to stay out of his father's way. Funny how he hadn't remembered that until he got here, funny how it all seemed to fade away.

At some point, he was going to have to eat something more substantial than stale Cheerios, but he put that in the category of *later* and returned to the living room. The backpack was just where he had left it, in the middle of the floor. *Who's paying attention now?* he almost said aloud, but didn't—a brief flash of restraint that made him feel momentarily lighter, as if his burdens had become diaphanous, little more than veils.

The backpack contained four items: a hatchet, a roll of duct tape, a rope, and a six-inch Bowie knife. *Like the pieces from a game of Clue,* he thought. *Junk bond trader in the basement with the hatchet. Ha, ha.* He had bought them all in Boston, in four separate locations, using cash. For a while, as he'd gathered materials, he had found himself dreaming through the situation, as if sleep had become less a matter of rest than of rehearsal, a kind of psychic run-through. He would see the house, the basement, the old man duct-taped to a kitchen chair. Or, at least, he thought it was the old man; in the dreams, he could never quite get close enough to tell. All he knew was that things had been reversed, that power lay in his hands.

As to what happened next, the dreams offered no oracle; he always woke up before the denouement.

The plan was simple: He was going to take the RTA to Chatham and kidnap the old man. Then, he would force him to drive back here, where he was going to exact an appropriately ruthless revenge. Downsizing, they had called it when the layoffs started. The company was downsizing. It was the type of corporate speak that drove him crazy: meaningless, a lie. His father had been a master of such double-talk, always saying the opposite of what he meant—*Why can't you be normal?* when the real question was why couldn't *he* be normal, why couldn't *he* be like the other dads? What was it that made him see in his son his own legacy of failure? What was it that made him attack? *It's a harsh world*, he liked to say, *I'm just trying to prepare you.* But this, of course, was just another lie.

Stop, he thought. *Forget about him. You've got bigger fish to fry.* He shook his head, trying to still the voices, took a deep breath, and exhaled. Backpack in hand, he went to the kitchen, grabbed a white wicker chair from the dinette set, and humped everything down the basement stairs. He had meant to come down here last night, but it had been so dark, and he had felt so buffeted by history . . .

It didn't matter. He was here now.

The basement had been cleaned out sometime during the last quarter century and left as empty space. For a moment, he was startled—there had been no photo on the realtor's website—but then he realized it was better, a template on which he could erase the past and write whatever future he wanted, not that there would be much for the old man. The idea was to get him down here and show him a new way to think about downsizing, to show him what a word like that really meant.

That was what the hatchet was for—to downsize the

old man digit by digit, limb by limb. That was why there was rope and duct tape, to keep him in the chair while his fingers, those greedy little fingers, were pared from him one by one. *Talk about severance*, he thought and laughed once, short and sharp. In the empty basement, it echoed like the barking of a dog.

He set the chair in a back corner and laid the hatchet and the rope and duct tape on the floor. The Bowie knife he rolled in his right hand. This, he was going to bring with him to Chatham; this, he was going to show the old man. *You're coming with me*, he would say, and then he'd stick him, just a little, not enough to hurt him but enough to break the skin. He could almost see it: a small pinpoint of blood, no bigger than a pimple, but at the same time, the biggest thing in the world. This would let the old man know he was serious, that it was his turn to be in charge. The old man would talk, trying to keep everything calm, trying to look for leverage, trying to make some kind of deal. Only later, when they got back here, would he realize that his bargaining days were behind him, and that all those things he'd valued—the suits, the cars, the houses—were forever out of reach.

First, though, he had to wait, just a few more hours, just until the afternoon. He went back upstairs, through the living room, to the second floor. At the top of the landing was the room in which he'd slept that summer, with two single beds and a pair of dressers, the same as when he'd been a kid. Standing at the door, he was aware of a low buzzing in his stomach, not exactly nerves or anticipation, but something almost like dread. *What makes you think you can do this? What makes you think you have the stones?* The words were his father's but the intonation was his own. *So that's what happens now?* he thought. *We blend together? That would be the cruelest fate of all.* The closet door was to his right, and he moved to it as if drawn. Inside, the space was tighter than he'd remembered, which made the whole thing somehow more unbearable, more treacherous, a small boy huddled in a narrow space, as if he were trying to remove himself from the world.

But no, he recalled now with a flash of recognition, that wasn't how it had happened. Yes, he'd been trying to remove himself, but only from his father, not from the world. After the door slammed, he had unfolded and drifted down the hall. From the bathroom, he had climbed onto the roof, slipped down to the woodshed, and quickly dropped to the ground. The day had been silent, except for the buzz of insects and the shushing of the surf. And the gasping of the wind in his ears as he ran for the jetty, where he'd spent the rest of the afternoon.

He looked in the closet again. He could almost see himself, but the image refused to coalesce. *Good*, he thought. *No more time for ghosts. No more time for anything.* But that wasn't true, not exactly, and in the few hours left before he went to Chatham, he knew where he wanted to go. He went downstairs, peered out into the morning to make sure no one was around. Satisfied, he let himself out of the house and headed for the beach path, to walk the jetty again.

Chatham was cold, and the old man's house overlooked the harbor, which made it colder still. He had timed it just right, disembarking at the rotary at five-fifty, full dark, staying to the shadows as he walked the empty streets. There were more year-rounders here, but that was fine; in a bigger town, it was easier to be anonymous. When he found the house, he walked right up to the front door and pressed the buzzer, not sure what he would do if no one answered, not sure what he would do if someone did.

As it turned out, it didn't matter because it was the old

man who came to the door. They stared at each other, near mirror images of surprise. "Excuse me?" said the old man, as if he couldn't place him, as if he weren't sure of who he was. Until then, there had been a conditional quality to the whole operation, as if, in spite of everything, he could turn around and take the RTA back to Harwichport, or even to Hyannis, and then another bus to Boston, leaving all of this—his plan, the vision, the bitter ghosts of that summer, of his father—behind. Now, as he watched the old man, smaller in corduroys and a sweater, he felt his anger catalyze. Laid me off, *downsized* me, and he doesn't know me? Without even thinking about it, he took the knife from his jacket pocket and pressed it into the old man's guts.

"You're coming with me," he said.

For a moment, it seemed as if the old man might cry out. Then he looked at the knife, gleaming in the lamplight, and steeled himself. "What is this?" he said. "What do you want?"

"Get your car keys. We're going for a ride."

The car was a Jeep Grand Cherokee, leather seats and all the extras, four-wheel drive and GPS. He gestured the old man into the driver's seat, keeping the knife against him, directed him back to the rotary and then east on Route 28. Along the way, they passed minimalls and seafood shacks, deserted as if summer would never come again. Just across the Harwich town line, a Chatham patrol car passed them going the other direction. He saw the old man's eyes flash quickly, watched his hands tighten on the wheel.

"Don't even think about it," he said, pushing the point of the knife blade into his side.

The old man didn't answer, just kept driving. After a moment, he whispered, in a voice less afraid than tired: "Please tell me what this is all about."

And then and there, he knew that he could never do it,

that he had fallen prey to inattention once again. He could almost hear his father, but they were too far from the house. What would he have said? *What makes you think you have the stones?* Yes, and that was true, wasn't it? Even sitting here in the car, knife in hand, felt like a weird sort of dream to him—or not a dream but a nightmare. Everything had gone according to plan, even better than the plan, and yet, he knew now, he was not going to see it through. How could he tie a man down and cut up his body? How had he imagined that he could? Delusion . . . but, of course, delusion was in his genes, it was the family way. *Right, Dad?* he thought with rising bitterness. *If I'm inattentive, what does that make you?*

The old man kept looking at him, as if waiting for an answer. They passed a restaurant and the Episcopal church. To their left, Wychmere Harbor opened up like a winter bloom, its basin devoid of boats.

"Pull over here," he said, gesturing at the empty parking lot of the ice cream shop.

The old man maneuvered into a parking space and turned off the Jeep. In the stillness, the engine ticked down like a clock. They sat for a minute, two minutes, until the ticking stopped. Time's up, he thought, game over; the clock has run out.

"You don't recognize me, do you?" he said to the old man. And then: "I've made a terrible mistake."

"Yes, you have," the old man replied. "As for the rest of it, I don't care."

"I used to work for you. You laid me off. Downsizing, you called it. But those were people's lives."

"*That's* what's going on here? You're a disgruntled employee? What are you planning to do? Hold me hostage until I give you your job back?" The old man looked at him, eyes as flat and gray as ice. "But that's not how the world works, is it?" he added, with a touch of cruelty. And the unraveling began.

The old man broke his gaze and opened the car door, sliding deliberately from the seat. The evening fragmented into a series of still images, black-and-white, stop-action, like a nickelodeon. First, he lunged at the old man, grabbing the sleeve of his sweater; it tore beneath his grasp. Then, he was getting out of the Jeep himself, heart beating frantically, breathing shallow, sweat pooling on his lower back and palms. "Wait!" he yelled. "What are you doing?"

At the sound of his voice, a light went on in the retirement home across the street. He was coming around the back of the Jeep when the old man pushed the panic button on his keyless entry, and the night exploded in a screech of honking and flashing lights.

"Motherfucker!" he shouted, and grabbed for the keys, but the old man was too fast. In one fluid gesture, he threw them into the scrub pines at the edge of the parking lot. The car alarm kept screaming, and more lights kept switching on. *No, no, no,* he thought. Then, without thinking about it or even meaning to, he was driving the knife hilt-deep into a gap between the old man's ribs.

The old man looked at him in silence; the old man never said a word. His face had a mocking look to it, as if, even now, a corona of blood expanding across the front of his sweater, he had somehow won. *Now what are you going to do?* he seemed to be saying. *You really didn't think this through.* Then he crumpled to the ground, slowly deflating, like an old balloon.

In a distant corner of the night, sirens rose and began coming closer, coming to where he was. He stared at the old man on the ground and understood he had to move. But something kept him there, a whisper of the moment past. It had only been a minute ago that none of this had happened; it seemed so close, he could almost reach out and grab it, like he had reached for the keys. Wasn't that what the ghosts had been trying to tell him, that nothing is ever lost, not really, that history accrues and lingers, marking the spaces we move through with its residue? If that was the case, why was this so irretrievable? Why was there no way to take it back?

The sirens were nearly on him now, and down Route 28 he could see the flashing of police lights. He cut across the street, hearing a shout of voices over the ongoing clamor of the alarm. He was running blind now, not even thinking in any conscious sense. All he knew was that he had to get inside.

At the house, he slipped along the driveway and through the back porch to the living room. It seemed like years since he had been here, since that summer maybe, when everything had begun. *You happy now?* he thought, or said aloud, he didn't know. *You happy now?* he thought again, and the noise was like a roaring in his head.

Outside, he could see flashlights. He went through the house, ending up in his old bedroom on the second floor. A bullhorn sounded, squawking words he did not care to hear. As if in a dream state, he opened the closet door and stepped inside, crouching low into the corner, willing himself to disappear.

He didn't know how long he stayed there, just that when he finally heard footsteps, he thought his father had come back. Then he heard the back-and-forth of voices and knew the cops were in the house. Again, without really thinking, he eased down the hall to the bathroom. It took a minute, but he opened the window and fought the screen out of its braces, giving access to the roof. Just like when he was thirteen, except that now his body felt so heavy he could barely bend it. Somehow, though, he managed to get outside, shoes slick on the wooden shingles, the ground a million miles below.

"Hey, you up there," a voice called out, and he was lit by a flashlight as he tried to work his way around. In his mind, a succession of phrases: *The human fly. Why can't you be normal? What makes you think you have the stones?* The light was blinding, and in its glare, he tumbled from the eaves to the woodshed, the flat roof breaking his descent. His back was screaming, ankle twisted, but the fall had freed him from illumination, and he took advantage of the darkness to make a mad dash for the only refuge that remained. Down the ocean path to the dunes and out to the water, sand filling up his shoes. Beneath the evening sky, the beach glowed silver, waves rolling along the surf line with the fury of high tide. Breathing heavily, he pulled himself toward the jetty. Behind him, voices and flashlights cut the night.

They had almost caught him when he reached the great stones of the breakwater and started out. But then, as he knew they would, they hesitated, giving him a second chance. He moved quickly, shoes slipping on the wet rocks, rough water pulling at his feet. Behind him, the officers had begun to follow carefully. He looked back at them, four men in a cluster, and understood, in a way he wouldn't have expected, that it was they who had been chasing him all along. He took a step back, and then another, thinking that he ought to turn around before he fell.

But as he pivoted, his twisted ankle buckled and he went down. He pulled himself to his knees just as a giant wave broke across the stones. The water was icy, full of needles, and as it pulled at him, he felt himself let go. He was aware of the roughness of the rocks as he scraped across them; he was aware of the beating of the air and ocean as the world went gray. He was aware of the policemen trying to reach him as he slid into the sea. But mostly, he was aware of the vision, aware of the ghosts. In his final seconds, he could see his father and the old man, faces looming like photographs. He could see himself as a boy, in this very spot, glimpsing his own death, he realized now. He could see his whole life whittled to a single instant. He had been here before.

THE OCCIDENTAL TOURIST

BY KAYLIE JONES

Dennis

L ast April we were waiting with our twelve-year-old daughter at the baggage carousel in Orlando, Florida, when the elderly couple standing beside us struck up a conversation. "Gee, the bags are taking forever," the wife said. "We never used to check them, but we're getting old." Her husband added that they'd been to Disney for their big anniversaries since they'd first discovered it with their kids. Were we going to Disney? Absolutely, said my husband with as much enthusiasm as he could muster—we'd resisted as long as we could. All during the flight, my husband had complained that for the same amount of money we could be scuba diving in Belize. "Oh you're going to love Disney World," the wife said. "Where you from?"

"New York City," I told them. They nodded knowingly, then the husband said they were from Charlestown, Mass. "Bet you never heard of it," he added with a devilish twinkle in his eyes.

Oh, I'd heard of it, all right. The Mile of Terror, the townies used to call it with profound pride. This was thirty years ago; more bars per capita than any other town in the United States. And the memories came flooding back. It was like finding an old shoebox in the very back of the very top shelf of the closet, filled with bright, sharp photographs.

Gavin McDermott was on a football scholarship at our Little Ivy League college in Connecticut. He was a Boston Irish Catholic boy from Dorchester. "You've heard of a mick," he'd say, "well I'm a BIC." Good thing he was proud of it because he couldn't have passed himself off as anything but. Tow-headed, blue-eyed, with a shovel-shaped Irish nose that reminded me of the snout on a great white shark, Mac had been a Golden Gloves champion in high school, and in college he was an extremely fast and enormously strong cornerback.

One night there was a big keg party at DKE, the fraternity of which he was president. I was standing at the basement bar drinking Mount Gay rum and pineapple juice when a DKE brother squeezed in beside me. "Liz, you'd better come quick, Mac and Sean McDermott are about to start fighting again." Sean, no relation, was from Chi Psi, the other Animal House frat on campus. The two McDermotts, who were no relation, had a long history of getting blotto and beating each other to a pulp; no one knew what had started it.

Though I didn't know the first thing about boxing, my father had also been a Golden Gloves champion, and then a pro for a while, and this, along with the fact that I typed Mac's English and social studies papers, often making corrections, was the foundation of our long and abiding friendship. I did not feel the slightest ripple of fear as I walked up to the two towering McDermotts, who stood nose to nose, eyes glistening madly, faces pale and tense, and told them to cut it out. Mac's eyes were blind with rage. For a second I thought he didn't recognize me. Then he backed away, mumbling, "Liz, you're nuts. One day you're going to get yourself killed."

No one knew, least of all me, why I had this effect on Mac. Once, when I wasn't there to talk him down, he kicked and punched in the windshield of some innocent car parked on the street and the police arrived en force, three squad cars with lights and sirens blaring. He hid in DKE's secret room, behind a wall in the basement, where they brought the pledges to meet the Witch. I knew this because I'd been the Witch during Pledge Week.

No one turned Mac in to the cops.

There were nine kids in his family and sometimes a few of them would come down from Boston to watch him play football on Saturday afternoons. His sisters looked so much like him that one of his DKE brothers beside me in the stands said, "What's Mac doing sitting in the bleachers in a fright wig?"

The summer of my junior year, after I got fired from my waitressing job in the Hamptons for telling off my boss, Mac invited me to visit "me and my buddies" on Cape Cod. He'd just graduated and had no idea what he was going to do come fall. For now, though, summer was in full swing and he was planning to play on the Cape as long as he could. "Coolest place you ever saw, Liz. I got a job as a bouncer in this nightclub in Dennis. Me and my buddies, we got it great. You can sit at the bar and drink all night for free. No one'll bother you."

My mom was in the south of France with a guy I couldn't stand. My dad died of a heart attack when I was a senior in high school; I knew long before he did that he should never have married my mother, a debutante who was looking to shock her parents. I weighed my options—south of France or Dennis, Mass. Never one to turn down a free drink, I took the Orient Point ferry to New London and drove up the coast in my old VW Rabbit, following the signs to the Cape. "There's only one road," Mac had said, "you can't get lost."

You couldn't get lost, but you could certainly get stuck in traffic. It was bumper to bumper all the way. I finally arrived around four in the afternoon.

Mac came out of the long, narrow clapboard house and sprinted down the short driveway to my car. He gave me a quick hug—never one for physical displays—and said, "Now,

Liz, these guys, they're from Charlestown," as if this was supposed to mean something to me. I waited. "They're a little
rough around the edges," he continued, "if you know what I
mean. They never saw a college like we went to." He winced
and cocked his head, a typical Mac expression that could mean
any number of things, but mostly that he was uncomfortable
with the topic and didn't want to discuss it further.

Inside the narrow house the cheap wood paneling made
the living room dark as a vault. Sitting upright on the wilted
couch was one of his sisters—Mary or Cathy—who especially
in the dark did look an awful lot like Mac in a fright wig. The
girls in the McDermott family were quiet; I don't think his
sisters ever said more than three words to me. I'd try, God
knows, to engage them in conversation, but they just wouldn't
talk. In any case, my attention was soon diverted; the house
was filled with people. One very pale fellow with mussed hair
sat hunched in a corner of the living room, beer in hand, legs
jiggling up and down. Every time the phone rang, he jumped
up out of his seat.

"What's wrong with *him?*" I asked.

"That's Bobby," Mac murmured as he showed me around.
The walls were thin, the doors made of hollow plywood. There
were three or four beds in every room. I had no idea where I
was going to sleep but I didn't want to make a point of bringing
it up. "Bobby had a little tussle a couple nights ago. He's kinda
laying low for the time being."

A typical Mac dysphemism. Next came the diversion:
"How about a cocktail?" He rubbed his hands together vigor-
ously and opened a kitchen cabinet.

I knew him well enough to stop asking questions. The
cabinet was filled with bottles, every kind of alcoholic bever-
age imaginable. Mac, bless his heart, had stocked up on Mount
Gay rum and pineapple juice.

By the time we got to the nightclub, I was feeling no pain. The place looked like a former warehouse, corrugated siding and tiny windows way up high. The bar was in the center of the cement floor and had four sides with the bottles stacked in the middle on shelves, so no one was at risk of ever having to wait too long for a drink. Within minutes of the doors opening, the place was jammed. Mac led me to an empty stool at the bar and sat me down, then went back to the door, where he was collecting the cover charge and barring unsavory types from entering.

One of the Charlestown roommates, Doyle, was behind my section of bar. There was a disco ball spinning in the background, projecting galaxies on the walls. People danced. I was careful not to wobble on the high stool and planted my elbows firmly on the shiny wood bar top. Doyle was missing a top incisor, which gave his face a strange, lopsided look. Every time he smiled or laughed, the black hole in his mouth was a shock. He liked to stick the filter of his menthol cigarette into the hole and leave it there while he puffed away, squinting against the smoke. He made sure my Mount Gay and pineapple juice never got below three-quarters empty. Earlier in the afternoon I'd watched him iron his jeans on a board in the living room, precisely and crisply, taking his time, making sure the crease was perfect. He wore a clean, ironed, button-down preppie shirt with the sleeves rolled up to his elbows. The music was so loud it was impossible to have a conversation, but a great deal could be communicated, simply by the delicate lighting of a cigarette or the pouring of a drink, or the replacing of a wet napkin, or the clinking of glasses in a toast. Doyle was good at his job, elegant and efficient. I tried to push a twenty-dollar bill toward him for the tip jar but he pushed it back without a word. They were hospitable, these Charlestown guys.

Every time a stranger approached me and tried to start up

a conversation or buy me a drink, Doyle would whisper some-thing in his ear and the fellow would scurry away. I gathered Gavin McDermott, guardian of the gates, had at some point gotten drunk here and lost his temper, just as he had in col-lege. Pretty soon I had a two-foot-wide berth around me, even though the place was packed like a subway car at rush hour. I was delighted with my new status.

When Doyle took his ten-minute break around back, I decided to join him. He was of medium height and very slim, with a dark, golden tan and pale brown hair and large, round eyes of an almost translucent cerulean green. I've only en-countered that eye color one other time, in a little girl in my daughter's ballet class. I mentioned how beautiful the color was to the girl's mother and she said they were from Estonia; the color was fairly common there.

But Doyle was from Charlestown, born and bred. Earlier in the day, while he was carefully ironing his jeans, he'd told me that the only place he'd ever been besides Boston was the Cape. Now, as we were leaning up against the corrugated metal wall of the nightclub around back, alone, blowing smoke up into the night sky, I asked him what happened with that guy Bobby. Why did he keep jumping out of his chair every time the phone rang? And why had he opted to stay at home alone tonight rather than come to the club?

"He got into it in the Combat Zone a couple nights ago with some guys that bat for the other team, if you get my meaning. He stabbed one a them and the guy died." Doyle's voice was even, as if he were discussing a friend's unfortunate and inconvenient ankle sprain. "Cops are looking for him."

I was trying to think through the fog of Mount Gay and pineapple juice. Didn't that make us guilty of aiding and abet-ting, or something? Harboring a criminal? I'd never met a mur-derer before. Was it my job to run to the closest pay phone and call the police? Mac would never speak to me again. And who was I to make that kind of decision? I was just visiting, I'd never seen this guy before. I liked Mac and I really liked this place, getting to sit in a prime spot at the bar all by myself, watched over by Mac and his friends. So I nodded at Doyle as if I understood exactly and let it go.

Doyle dropped his mentholated butt on the dried seashell-covered ground and stepped on it. "Mac is in love with you," he said in a neutral tone, and walked back toward the door.

"It's not like that between us," I protested, wanting to explain, but when Doyle opened the door the music hit us like a detonation. It was useless to pursue the conversation.

"Mac doesn't pick up girls," Doyle said sometime later, during another break. We were smoking out back again. "He's not, I guess, relaxed about sex, would be my estimation. He's a different kind of tense around you."

All these years we'd been friends and Mac had never made a pass at me. "I don't have a clue what you're talking about!" I countered, sounding for a moment just like my mother.

"You're a rich girl, aren't you?" Doyle said with a smile, sticking a fresh cigarette into the black gap between his teeth. I'd never before met anyone with an incisor missing. I couldn't take my eyes off it.

"My mother was a debutante," I replied with a nervous chuckle.

"What's a debutante?"

I laughed. He leaned forward and kissed me, all menthol breath and vodka and orange juice. We'd been keeping up, matching each other one for one, all night.

In the wee hours of the morning, after the nightclub closed, I wanted to go to an after-hours party with Doyle but Mac pulled me away and drove me back to the house. Bobby the wanted murderer was nowhere to be seen. I was sitting on the faded, wilted couch, when Mac leaned in awkwardly to kiss me. I tried to push him away with both palms. His eyes slipped out of focus, became glazed with rage; I recognized the look and felt a tremor of fear before defiance kicked in.

"Don't you know how you make me feel?" he muttered between clenched teeth. "You know, don't you? You know."

"To hell with you, Mac," I said, and in a flash he was on top of me. I struggled to free myself; I felt like I was lying under a refrigerator. He got his hands around my neck and started to choke me. Doyle came through the front door just as I was losing consciousness and he lifted the cheap trunk that they used as a coffee table and whacked Mac with it on the back of the head.

Doyle pulled me up to sitting, Mac out cold on the floor beneath us. "You all right? He could've killed you."

I rubbed my neck, trying to catch my breath. "It's weird," I said, "at the time, I didn't really care. I guess I'm drunker than I thought."

While Mac slept it off, Doyle and I walked around the neighborhood of one-story houses. We sat down on someone's lawn, which was slightly pitched. It was very dark. "Sometimes Mac gets violent when he drinks too much," Doyle explained, as if he were talking about his aging uncle's blood pressure. "It's like a switch goes off in his head. You can see it in his eyes. Tomorrow he won't remember."

"I know," I said. "Everyone always protected him at school. What'll happen to him now that he's back in the real world?"

"Everyone will keep on protecting him."

We talked for a long time. There were no stars in the sky; the clouds had rolled in as they often do near the beach at night. I told him about my mother and her awful boyfriend, gambling and partying in the south of France. I told him about how my dad died alone, drunk and broken, in a flophouse in upstate New York. Even I had walked away from him, and he'd been the only person I ever loved. I explained to Doyle that sometimes being on the move seemed best. Four years of college was the longest I'd ever stayed in one place. But I knew the only chance I had was to finish, and to keep on learning. Reading and reading until I knew so much no one could hurt me. I didn't know who I was or where I was going but I knew I had to keep on learning. I told Doyle these things I had never told a soul, feeling his warmth and his breath beside me but not able to see him. He told me he had a girlfriend who was in a Charlestown gang called the Stingers, all girls. He said if she ever found out he'd fallen in love with someone in ten minutes flat, she'd cut us both up, but good.

"Is Doyle your first or last name?"

"Last. My name is Bill—but no one calls me Bill except my parents."

The darkness gradually began to fade around us. I saw the house's mailbox take shape, a set of lines forming a silvery rectangle in the darkness. Then I noticed the watery rose-colored sunlight on the wet grass; dew had soaked through our clothes. The pale green color of the grass was the same as his eyes.

"You have the most beautiful eyes," I told him. And kissed him again for a long time.

"We better get back," Doyle finally said. By now the sun was shining brightly and I felt dizzy and exposed. The birds had started chirping, making a racket. We walked back through the deserted neighborhood, all the houses one-story summer rentals set out in orderly crescents, with little square lawns.

When we walked into the house, Bobby was packing up his stuff. He said he was driving back to Boston to turn himself in.

He didn't have much, an old backpack filled with dirty clothes. He was shoving socks in a side pocket. He said hiding out was too much for his nerves. Waiting all night for the cops to show up. It was an accident, he told us, as if he were practicing for his interrogation. He never meant to hurt the guy. It was self-defense, he added, suddenly inspired.

He hesitated at the door, shuffling his feet. "Well, later then," he murmured, and disappeared.

Mac had gone into one of the bedrooms to sleep off his drunk. He would either not remember or pretend it had never happened; that was his way.

I decided I should go also; perhaps the south of France was a better idea, after all. Doyle walked me to my car and leaned in through the driver's-side window as I rolled it down. "Just know this," he said. "This isn't over."

He wrote his phone number in Charlestown on a corner of my map and I gave him my mother's phone and address in the city. I promised to call him as soon as I got back to college and had a number of my own. He tapped the roof of the Rabbit lightly a couple of times, and I drove off.

While I was a senior in college and then a graduate student at Columbia, I would go up to Boston on occasion to see him. Once, we rented a motel room off the interstate, and another time we spent a warm spring afternoon driving around Charlestown in my VW Rabbit, Doyle behind the wheel. The Mile of Terror, the townies called it. He showed me Bunker Hill. No one was home at the apartment where he'd been born—the Doyles didn't trust hospitals, he explained—and he still lived with his family on Dunstable Street, in a complex of two-story condominiums with gray aluminum siding, all the units exactly alike. In the living room, on the wall above the gas fireplace, hung a family portrait of all six Doyles: father, mother, three sisters, and Bill, sitting in a field of flowers with an unlikely blue sky and white puffy clouds overhead. The artist had painted in Doyle's missing tooth.

He told me that night in another motel room that he was thinking of taking a trip across the country. I never found out if he went.

Many months later, when I was beginning my serious downward spiral, Doyle called me one morning in my apartment near Columbia.

"I got a big favor to ask you. If you can't do it, just say so. I need three hundred dollars," he said. "I got a debt to pay."

"Who do you owe?" I asked.

"Filene's Basement. I ran up a credit card."

I wasn't rolling in money, but it wouldn't be a hardship to give it to him. "How do you want me to send it to you? Is a check okay, or do you need cash?"

"I can cash a check in the bar where I work." After a pause, he added, "Thank you, Liz. I knew you'd come through, and I'll never forget it. If you ever need anything, you know where I am."

A year passed and I was working nights as a temp in a law firm, trying to finish law school. I was sort of seeing a guy I'd met in the Marlin, a bar on 110th and Broadway, around the corner from my apartment. Drinking close to home, it was easier to stay out of trouble. Joe Giorno had a black mustache and a Datsun 280z and lived in Hoboken. He worked for a moving company and dealt a little cocaine to Columbia students on the side. He said dealing coke was a lot easier and more lucrative than humping furniture around the city. One night we were in his 280z on our way to his place in Hoboken when he said he had to make a little detour. He drove down a street in the West 40s, slowing as we passed a parked car. There was a guy behind the wheel who wasn't moving, his head thrown back and his mouth wide open. There was a muddy smear of blood on the window.

"Shit," Joe said. Then he turned to me: "If anybody asks, I was with you all night, you understand? All night."

I dug Doyle's phone number out of an old address book and called him as soon as I got home the next morning.

"Doyle," I said, and he knew who it was. I started crying. He asked me for the details calmly, like a doctor listening to a patient's symptoms. He wanted Joe's full name and exact address.

"I'll make some calls," he said. "Don't worry about it anymore. But Liz, listen to me. If anybody comes looking for you, get up here as fast as you can. You'll be safe here."

I never again heard from Joe Giorno. No one ever came looking or asking questions. He was gone, as if he'd never existed. I stopped hanging out at the Marlin.

Doyle sent me a card on my fortieth birthday, to my mother's New York City address. By then I'd moved around the city many times. By then I'd also been sober for nine years. The card had a bottle of French wine on the cover and the inside read, *You're just like wine, you get better with time.* He'd signed the card, *Love, Doyle.*

Standing in the Orlando airport waiting for our luggage with the elderly couple from Charlestown who loved Disney World, I considered asking them if they knew the Doyles on Dunstable Street. But there were probably hundreds of Doyles in Charlestown, and I did not remember his parents' first names, if I'd ever known them at all.

Later, in the rental car driving to Disney World, while our daughter slept sprawled across the backseat, I thought about telling my husband the story. But that girl no longer exists, and my husband has never met her. He's never seen me drunk. He doesn't know about Mac, or Bobby huddled in that Cape Cod living room, how close I came to the edge. I am now a mother who takes her daughter to Disney World, married to a man who does the same.

I think of Doyle still, and my heart feels warm as I send good thoughts his way. From time to time I feel him thinking about me, and wonder how he's faring.

PART III

END OF THE LINE

THE EXCHANGE STUDENT

BY FRED G. LEEBRON

Provincetown

The news started coming down Route 6 early that Saturday morning, a peculiar siren sound like a cross between a busy phone signal and an overworked synthesizer. It blasted into the house at 8:32 a.m. when the exchange student was woken by high-pitched keening from the downstairs kitchen.

His eyes raced around the still strange bedroom. His half-full blue rucksack leaned in a corner, his Danish-English dictionary sat on a dark pine desk. He felt under the bed for his unpacked suitcase. Was it keening or was it wailing? He knew he should stay in his room until it passed. It became guttural, as if the voice were choking, and the only words he could understand were: "Now, now . . ." Doors were opening and closing all over the house. There was sobbing. He thought hard to the last time he had heard such emotion. There wasn't a time. The reputation of New Englanders was that they were restrained, deeply reticent, until you got to know them, and that often took a good while. Even then, sometimes, you wouldn't catch so much as a grin or a tear. He lay in bed. His new watch, waterproof to a depth of fifteen feet, told him that an hour had passed. An hour!

It was only August. He still had eleven months left, if he were counting, which he was not. He was just trying to endure. His American brother frequented the gay discotheques, his American sister thought she must be far prettier than she was, his American father was a gnarled pontificator (about what wasn't yet clear to the exchange student) missing a thumb—he ran a whale watching company—and his American mother seemed as old and stunted as his grandmother back home. Three weeks ago, when he'd seen this unlikely group at South Station in Boston along with all the other host families, he'd prayed they weren't his—and he never prayed.

Now it was 10:05 and the house was silent. It was always difficult to know when to appear and when to disappear. His room was tucked away in a far upper corner, and he could be as invisible as they needed him to be. He supposed he could use the bathroom.

His trip took him past his sister's room, which was empty, and to his brother's door, which was thrown open to the usual mess of cassettes and records. His brother liked to quiz him on music and was appalled by his limited knowledge.

The bathroom was pleasant and white and warm. It caught the morning sun through a skylight. He wondered where everyone was and what the hell had happened. When he was finished, he went into the hallway and looked out the window onto the driveway. Empty. It was a Sunday morning and everything was recovering from the havoc of an August Saturday night and there wasn't a single car. He felt a strange thrill when he realized he might be alone.

He tiptoed down the stairs—he was of course already dressed, you couldn't go to the bathroom without being dressed—and opened the living room door. A newspaper had been left open on the green leather couch. A cup of coffee sat unfinished on a side table. He crossed to the kitchen. On the bare table was a note: *Help yourself to food.*

Hesitantly, he opened the refrigerator. There was milk and cheese and eggs and something they called *linguica*, plus a plastic container of cream cheese. On the counter were a jar of jam and a bag of rolls from the Portuguese bakery and a bottle of fizzy water. He poured himself some fizzy water and sat at the breakfast table.

The phone rang. He'd never answered it before. It rang and rang and rang. He looked at it; it was black with a rotary dial and appeared ancient. Was it ringing for him? He waited through the twentieth ring and then picked up.

"Good morning," he said.

A man's voice poured back at him, rushed and elusive.

In his best American, he told the man that he didn't speak American so well.

The man offered a few choice words about that—what they were was anybody's guess—and hung up.

He took the glass of fizzy water out through the living room to the front hall and opened the door to the driveway. He stood there smelling the salt air. Carefully he searched the sky above the pine trees that surrounded their partially settled neighborhood, cut off by Route 6 from the town. Just last week on a dune hike, they'd seen a shack practically spontaneously combust. What the hell was going on here?

Against the wall of the house leaned a lone motorbike. That would be his once Valerie left for Denmark. He looked at his watch—he'd never had a watch before—and saw that would be in just two days. In just two days he'd be free of her. She spoke to him more than anybody else in the family, but primarily it all revolved around how many boys kept telling her how beautiful she was. She was all right, but she was not beautiful. She had dark hair, for one thing. He couldn't tell whether she was trying to provoke him into saying something like, *But you are beautiful,* or if she was just gloating. The town had never had an exchange student before, inbound or outbound. The silence was unstinting.

A car pulled into the driveway, spraying pebbles and

seashells. Valerie and her parents were visible through its smudged oversized windows. He waved to them uncertainly. What was he supposed to do—go to the car, retreat into the house, stand there like a statue? Finally, Valerie got out of the car. She strode over to him and took his hand. She was an inch or two taller.

"Come," she said with grim determination.

She led him into the house and through the kitchen to the refrigerator, still holding his hand. She'd never held his hand before. He wasn't surprised that he didn't like it. She opened the refrigerator and grabbed two cans of beer and shut the door with her hip and led him upstairs. At the top of the stairs she looked left and right, as if she'd never been there before. "Okay, okay," she said, urging herself onward, still holding his hand. She'd probably held a lot of hands. He wondered if she'd had sex yet; he hadn't, though of course it was never far from his mind.

They walked down the hall together, separately but side by side. He thought he could see a tear in the corner of her eye; he thought he could sense something awful waiting at the end of the hall. She opened the door to his room, pulled him in, shut it, sat him forcefully on the bed, sat beside him, opened a can and handed it to him, opened her can, and tried to smile.

"Skaal," she said, perhaps her one word of Danish, tapping his can with hers.

"Skaal," he said.

She took a sip and he took a sip.

"What have you been doing this morning?" she asked. "What have you heard?"

He looked at her. It seemed wrong, perhaps even dangerous, to admit he'd heard anything. "I was asleep," he said.

"You couldn't sleep through that." She looked at him in frank disbelief.

"I don't know what I heard."

She took up his hand again; at a point, he didn't know when, she'd ceased holding it. "What you heard was my mother crying because my brother has been killed in a car accident."

As the words left her mouth, her face crumpled as if it had forgotten it had bones. Tears streamed from her clenched eyes. He reached for her because that was all he could think to do, and both their cans spilled and fell to the carpeted floor. Her chest heaved against his and he willed himself not to grow hard and was relieved to see that the effect at least for the moment followed the intent.

"Ronnie," she sobbed. "Oh, Ronnie!"

He knew he should express some feeling, but he also knew that it would seem false because it *was* false, and he had so little experience on this front that any gesture was risky. Holding her, as he continued to hold her, was risky. He remembered glimpsing his mother through her half-open bedroom door when she'd come home from the hospital after Grandfather had died, and stepping carefully into her room and going right up to her and hugging her and saying, "Oh, I'm so sorry, I'm so sorry," and how that had been the right thing to do.

"Oh, I'm so sorry. I'm so sorry," he said to Valerie.

She was sobbing and sniffling, trying to get on top of the emotion and falling right through it so that she was all emotion and nothing else. He rubbed her back in what he hoped was a brotherly way.

"My mother," she forced out. "Will. Not. Ever. Get. Over. This."

It was too early in his stay for him to know anyone's story. The routine had been a leisurely but efficient breakfast, a drive to this new place or that—Race Point, his future school now just eight days away, the A&P out Shank Painter, the odd thick forest that grew just south of where the dunes ended, the little Provincetown airport—then lunch at home, time alone in his room to study English, afternoon coffee in the living room, dinner, more time alone in his room, evening television and evening coffee in the den, polite and grateful goodnight. (At the two-week language school prior to their distribution to their host families, the exchange students had been bludgeoned with the fact that the most important single phrase in New England was *thank you*, and he said it these days, by his count, at least twice an hour, to everything—meals, coffee, being told where the extra soap was kept, being taken along to the supermarket, being brought home from the supermarket, being irrecusably invited to go sit in the gay discotheque for seven hours practically every Friday and Saturday night, the beer occasionally slid his way, being told there was a letter from home.) All he knew was that Ronnie and Valerie were Americans by birth, that they'd been adopted, that they'd been teased in school mercilessly about it, that Valerie had absolutely zero curiosity about her birth mother but knew her to be a drunk (they'd met once), that Ronnie, while working regular hours in his father's whale watching company, was desperate to be a deejay and travel around the States and maybe to Canada, that he really didn't know these people and didn't necessarily want to, that this was the longest, strangest embrace of his life.

Soon, she stopped trembling and signaled, very deftly he thought, almost like a shrug, that she was ready to release. Quickly, he opened his arms and she shifted slightly away and arched her back and looked at the floor.

"Oh. Those beers," she said.

He moved to get something to address them.

"Don't," she said. "Don't do anything, okay?"

She rubbed at her eyes as if she could shut off her tear ducts. She reached into the pocket of the lightweight black leather jacket she always wore and pulled out a pack of cigarettes.

"Do you mind?" she asked.

"Of course not."

She went to the window and popped it open and lit the cigarette with her red plastic lighter and stood smoking into the fresh still air. She smiled coldly at him, shaking her head.

"I could use a beer," she said. "Mom and Dad, I don't know when they'll be back, but it will be hours before she'll want to come home, and I'm not sure what it is I should be doing."

He stayed on the bed, nodding, remembering her instruction not to do anything.

"This will be very difficult for you," she said.

She was still looking at him. He nodded. Again, he didn't want to say anything inauthentic, it was too big a situation not to say anything completely true, and he had no idea what the complete truth was. That *he* didn't matter? Well that was a lie, that couldn't be what he thought, selfless thoughts were rarely true, at least from his experience. Good God, this *was* going to be hard.

"Can't you say anything?" she demanded.

"There is nothing good to say," he tried.

"Well, that's something." She reached through the window and crushed the cigarette against the side of the house and then must have let it drop to the ground because when she pulled her hand back in, it was empty. She stepped past the spilled cans and took his hand.

"Let's get a beer," she said.

Jens, that was his name, Jens, he didn't really know how much he'd figure into this story so he hadn't yet taken a name, Jens walked with her down the empty hall and now it was like he too had never been here before, everything suddenly seemed so different, the hallway wider or narrower, the walls brighter or darker, he couldn't tell. Even though he hadn't cried, hadn't shed a single tear, he felt as if he had. He felt wrung out. Maybe he felt stoned. Not quite paranoid, but approaching it, as if the floor might at any minute be taken out from under him, and he'd like to be prepared. Valerie held his hand all the way down the stairs and into the kitchen and even as she rummaged through the refrigerator. She must have felt the same way. It was an awful feeling. For the first time since he'd left home he found himself nearly missing his parents.

"What are you thinking?" she asked as they stood in the kitchen sipping beer, no longer holding hands.

"Nothing," he said.

It was odd how he didn't miss his parents. None of the other exchange students missed theirs either, or one did, but she'd already gone back home. They were an odd, slightly estranged lot, and next year, though of course he didn't know this yet, when he went to university with a whole other group of people, he'd discover that they too were an odd, slightly estranged lot. It made sense of course—or it would make sense—but still.

"That's a lie," Valerie said.

"Of course it's a lie," he said. "Anytime anyone says they're thinking nothing, it's a lie, because everyone's always thinking something." He looked at his beer, surprised. Had he really just said that?

"Exactly," Valerie said.

They took small sips of their beers in rapid succession, as if they couldn't bear to have their mouths freed from the bottles, because then what would they say? Valerie turned to stare out the window onto the empty driveway.

"My God, you are going to be here all alone," she said to the window. "I have to go, you know. It means everything to my dad that I go. And I want to." Her back still to him, she brushed quickly at her face.

"They're saying he was drunk," she continued. "But what does that matter? He didn't hurt anyone but himself. When we went to see him his face was all blue and swollen but he did, as they say, look peaceful." Then she let loose a stream of words and he had no idea what she was saying, except for the curse words, which Ronnie had been teaching him diligently.

She turned back and her face was flecked with tears and splotched.

"We're stuck here, you know. There's no car and only one motorbike and it's too small for two of us and there's nowhere really I want to go and I was told not to leave you by yourself anyway. Are you afraid?"

"Afraid?" Sure, he was afraid, but he didn't yet know of what. But yes, he could feel some fear. It was in his stomach, the way he felt kind of sick.

"Afraid," she said. "Can you say that? Say, *Are you afraid.*"

"Are you afraid."

"Yes," she said. "I am."

That he understood.

"Really," she said.

"Of what?"

"Oh." She let out a long sigh, like she was trying to gather herself and it wasn't him she wanted to talk to anyway. "You know what, I'm really tired. I really don't know what I'm saying."

She finished her beer and stared at him until he finished his. Then she reached in and got them two more.

"I don't know where we should sit," she said. Clearly, the task of him had been assigned to her, and that evidently involved sitting somewhere in a civilized fashion. "This house is too damn big now. Is it okay if we stay in the kitchen?"

"Of course," he said, marveling at how steady he sounded. She was two years older and an inch or two taller, and usually when he was with her he felt about twelve. Twelve or thirteen. Now she leaned against the dry sink and he leaned against the counter and they sipped their beers just once. He looked at the floor, he couldn't look at her anymore, it was too hard, it hurt to look at her, like it was wrong to look at her, like really she needed to be however she could be and not have to be looked at. A single American ant traveled along over the American kitchen floor, weighted by a speck of a bread crumb.

"You didn't even really know him, did you? You don't really know any of us."

"Yes," he answered, but it came out a whisper, an intake of breath. That was the way the Danes said yes, breathing in at the same time as the word came out. It was meant as a form of encouragement, used mostly to signal to the one who was talking to keep going.

She looked at him queerly. "What the hell was that?"

"My . . . my breathing slipped."

A laugh escaped her mouth and she immediately covered it with a hand. Her eyes had a certain brightness even though they were brown, and her brown curly shoulder-length hair fell wherever it wanted. Her face was pale and thin and narrow, and her chin came to a delicate point. He hadn't seen her laugh by mistake before.

"What are you looking at?" she asked without accusation.

He felt his face redden. Was this really happening, or would he wake up soon? That was the way it usually worked. He didn't masturbate—he supposed his parents had somehow kept him from it before he was truly conscious of the possibility; they'd somehow conditioned him—and so he had wet dreams, lots of them, and lately, unfortunately, they involved Valerie and he always woke right after it was too late to stop whatever was happening to him.

"Sorry," he said. He looked at her with true apology and

she smiled back at him without any threat or meaning what-soever, as if maybe she didn't even know what he was sorry for.

"You have trouble sleeping, don't you?" she observed. "Al-most every night I hear you get up and go to the bathroom."

How did these people appear to know everything, when he knew nothing? Had he run the water so long that she could tell he was cleaning himself up? She seemed to be mocking him in that way she sometimes couldn't help but have, the way that said, *I have all the experience and you will never have any*. His face felt so hot he could no longer feel it.

"You don't look so good," she said, and he couldn't tell whether she was amused or concerned or both. How could anyone be both? How could Ronnie be dead and they be standing here drinking beer on such an eerie Sunday morn-ing? Suddenly, she reached across and felt his forehead, rested her hand there. "You're hot," she said, and took her hand away matter-of-factly. "God, everything's so crazy I don't know how it can all be real." She wiped one eye and then the other. He glanced around and down at the floor. "Maybe we could sit on the floor? I don't know how to explain it but I don't want to sit in the breakfast nook." Her hand waved at the arrangement.

"Nook," he said.

"Yes, breakfast nook. That's what it's called." She sat on the floor cross-legged. Gingerly, as if he thought he might in-jure himself, he sat down across from her.

"I've never done this before," she said, "but for the first time I think I'm glad we have a small kitchen." She sipped her beer. "I feel like we're little kids."

He nodded and drank seriously from his beer, or he nod-ded seriously and drank from his beer. It was only his second and really watery, but he was seventeen and he weighed fifty-five kilos and he hadn't eaten since yesterday evening's din-ner, when they had squeezed into the "nook" and Ellen had brought her chair out to sit at the head and they had the usual ground beef and ketchup and something that was green like broccoli or kale. Then Ellen had done the dishes with Valerie and he had sat in the living room with Ralph and Ronnie and they had read the *Cape Cod Times* and he had read his book— he was trying to read a lot for his English, to ease himself into the swing of things when really he was just depressed, waiting for school to begin, waiting for his new life to begin. He was reading *The Source*, wondering what relics might possibly be found in the apparently thin ground beneath them, and then it was time for coffee and television in the den where they watched their favorite series, M*A*S*H, which was helping him to learn. It had a lot of sarcasm in it, every episode featured several sarcastic exchanges, and he was amazed by how the family looked at it so normally, as if there was nothing obvious about it, and after it was over, Ronnie had said, "I'm going out for a drive." He'd turned to Jens and punched him lightly on the shoulder and said, "You want to come?" and Jens had stopped his face from souring at the thought of another too dark and too fast ride to one of Ronnie's friends' houses, where they'd sit in the mildewed basement and listen to Donna Summer and Boney M. and have one watery beer or at most two beers each and he'd have to nod his head to the music and pretend he liked it. "No, thank you," he'd said, "but thank you." They all laughed at him at that, and Ronnie said, "Crazy Dane," and batted him on the shoulder, and shook his keys in his hand like dice, and said, "See you." The remaining tufts of his dirty-blond hair had fluttered as he hurried from the house. In the den, Valerie had rolled her eyes and shook her head, and he couldn't tell whether it was at him for not going or at Ronnie for, well, being Ronnie.

"Now what are you thinking about?" Valerie asked.

"Last night," he said.

"I was going to tell you about Ronnie and me as little kids, but I don't want to talk about the past." Suddenly she rose and brushed herself off. "We should have a drink."

He went with her to the cabinet in the living room where the hard stuff was kept. She got two little glasses and handed them to him, then took out a dark bottle and looked at it and returned it to the cabinet and then took out another one and inspected it.

"This one, I think," she said, holding it up to him. "I don't think you've tried this one yet."

"Okay," he said, though the thought of anything strong and fiery going down his throat and into his empty stomach nearly set him on the floor again.

"I think maybe we're going too slowly. I think maybe we should be drinking faster," she muttered almost to herself. "Where did we leave our beers?"

"On the kitchen floor. I'll get them."

"No—"

But he was past her and entering the kitchen, where he promptly kicked over both cans.

"That's four." She clapped her hands as if he were a zoo animal who had performed this feat unwittingly for her entertainment, which seemed to him probably correct. "Soon we'll be swimming in beer. Soon the whole house will be flooded with beer."

"I am so sorry," he said, blushing, looking for a paper towel. He wasn't sure they had paper towels in this country. "Excuse me."

She set the cans on the table and reached out and he handed over the shot glasses. "We'll have a shot and then we'll clean this and then we'll clean upstairs. We have so much time."

"I am such an idiot," he said, his face hotter than ever.

"We've come to expect it." She patted him in a motherly fashion on his shoulder, three quick taps, then poured the shots. She peered at him and raised her glass. "To Ronnie," she said, her expression instantly contorting and then returning to itself.

"To Ronnie," he said.

When he downed the shot, it was like a blowtorch in the face. The shock ran up his nose and down his throat and spine and burned his stomach like it harbored lighter fluid.

"Very good." She set down the glass and started wiping up the beer.

He reached around her narrow shoulders and plucked up the cans and stepped over the puddle and jammed them into the garbage can under the sink.

"You see," she said, showing him the freshly dried floor. "It's nothing. Can you hand me a wet paper towel with a little soap on it?"

He found the paper towels and soaked one with warm water and a little soap and handed it to her, making sure their fingers didn't touch.

"You are such a careful boy, even when you're not."

There was a candid assessment in her words but also blunt despair. All those times he'd gone with Ronnie, five or six times in just three weeks, the guy never had more than two beers. He preferred drinking in the discotheque or in his room. Had Ronnie gone to the discotheque without Valerie and him?

"Now what are you thinking about?" Valerie asked, looking up from the floor where she rested on one hand, legs folded under her. The upward turn of her face and the upward cast of her eyes made her appear surprisingly like a lost child, mouth slightly open and lips parted as if she wanted to say something more but had no idea what it was and was waiting for him to say something too. He felt queasy and bereft, as if the floor had indeed decided to shift from underneath him.

"I'm going to miss you," he said.

"I know." She gave one last wipe and stood up and stepped right next to him at the sink, where she rinsed and wrung out the cloth and set it on the counter. "Now we have to deal with upstairs." She dried her hands on her jeans and reached out for him and he gave up his hand, and when she held it he felt on slightly firmer ground.

On the way upstairs, she grabbed a small towel from the bathroom and soaked it and soaped it and then led him to his room, where she dropped to her knees. He reached around her again and picked up the cans and started for the kitchen.

"Don't leave me up here alone," she said.

Her tone, so simple and yet so starkly and unbearably vulnerable, startled him and he halted instantly as if jerked by a rope, and then he was falling, falling on his clogs—that was the first thing Ralph and Ellen had remarked about him, that he wore those clogs—and he tumbled out of them onto the floor. She was laughing so hard her face was red. She let the towel fall and crawled to him and held him in her arms against her lap and breasts as if he were some kind of fallen soldier.

"Is my little Dane hurt?" she said, and kissed him on the forehead. She withdrew for a moment as if trying to convince herself of something, and he was still gazing at her thinking this must be a dream, don't do anything, don't do anything, when she bent again and kissed him with her tongue, without pause, she could actually breathe while kissing him and he was trying to kiss her back. Then she was moving from under him and was over him and on top of him on the floor and her hand was sweeping his chest, gliding down toward his jeans, and unzipping him, all seemingly in one movement, and they were still kissing and he was still telling himself don't, don't, and thinking don't what? Don't let her do this in her state or don't come yet or what? And she was all over him and he was kissing her and just holding on tight and he was out of his pants and underwear and she was out of her pants and underwear and his hand was under her jacket and shirt—she still had that jacket on!—and she was straddling him and then something happened and he couldn't help himself. He said, "Am I in?"

"Haven't you done it before?"

"Of course," he said.

And she was moving atop him and he was thinking about how lucky he was on such an unlucky day and he was thinking it felt different than he thought it would and he was thinking he was starting to ache a little, that somehow it was starting to hurt.

"You're supposed to too," she said.

"What?"

"Move."

Move how? he thought. The truth was he didn't know. He'd seen parts of some porn films, but they were kind of gross and he hadn't learned anything from them. He moved sideways.

"What *are* you doing?"

"Moving," he said, and he worried it came out like a question.

Then her face collapsed and she was crying, really crying, her chest wracked with sobs, and she sank fully upon him, and then she slid from him and lay atop him weeping and her face was pressing against his shirt and he didn't know where to put his hands—certainly not on her bare bottom—and he held her tightly through her leather jacket and she cried and cried.

After a while she stopped and her hand found him again, and again she slid him into herself and was moving with an almost seriousness of purpose.

"Why are we doing this?" he asked.

"Shut up," she said. "Just be quiet. Okay?"

He knew enough not to say even okay. She kept going and he was trying to move somehow—how could he be so ignorant about this, so unknowing?—and then she swallowed hard and her eyes didn't appear to be looking at all, and she stopped and patted him lightly on the chest.

"Okay," she said.

She maneuvered herself off him and stood and went to the bed for the duvet and came back and lay beside him on the floor and covered them both because it did seem suddenly colder than it was.

"You'll be so much different when I come back in a year," she said. "You'll know how. The girls here have never seen a Dane and they'll be curious."

And neither of them could know—how could they?—that she wouldn't come back in a year but in two and a half months, because it would turn out to be so awful over there, so horrible, in silly backward small-town Denmark, and her face would be so haggard and gaunt that she'd look at least thirty, sitting across from him in the breakfast nook as she smoked her cigarettes and rolled her eyes. And he couldn't know and she couldn't know that in just twenty years both her parents would be in the ground and she would be in the ground, that they would all be dead, leaving nobody behind except maybe him and he didn't count.

He could feel her groping around and she dug out a cigarette from her jacket pocket and lit it and lay on her back smoking up at the ceiling.

"You know, we talked about it," she said.

"What?"

"Ronnie and I. We talked about doing it. Fucking. I mean, we weren't—" her voice caught at that. "Weren't related, really. So we could have. And we talked about it. But we didn't do it."

"Oh." For an instant, he had a vision of them doing it and it made him shiver.

"Is my little Dane cold?" She moved a hand toward him. "My little Dane who'd never done it before."

"I know," he admitted.

"You're going to be fine," she said.

And he was, he was going to be fine. Although they wouldn't ever sleep together again, he would last the year and go to university and marry and have kids and, in all the ordinary meanness and tragedy of life, experience happiness. But none of them here in this house would experience that after today. Yesterday would be their last day. The police would determine that Ronnie wasn't drunk, he just hadn't been a particularly cautious driver. He liked to go really fast. Jens could remember that, how the trees whistled at them on their way to Race Point, how Ronnie turned Province Lands Road into his personal quarter oval. He could remember sitting in the passenger seat and thinking it was so dangerous he couldn't even admit to himself just how terrified he was, the way Ronnie would look over at him grinning insanely but in a not unkind fashion as he brought the car up to ninety and then one hundred miles an hour, his zany American brother.

But that was a long time ago, before many of you were even born. Don't think about it, there's no point in thinking about it. There's no point in trying to look back.

VIVA REGINA

BY BEN GREENMAN
Woods Hole

I was minding my own business.

I was at home watching television.

The show was a police drama.

Everyone told me that it was fantastic.

I didn't see the appeal.

The older detective was always shouting at the younger detective.

The younger detective was always champing at the bit to solve the cases quickly.

Their female sergeant wore her uniform comically tight.

The show was set in Boston and the accents were broad.

I couldn't keep track of anyone's names.

I had started with the sense that I would watch the entire hour and while I did my best I was soon overcome with fatigue and I started to lean back into the couch and consequently into sleep.

I was so tired I thought I would never be alert again.

I could not afford to be tired.

I had too much to do.

I needed to stay awake.

That was the first thing I had to do.

I went out for a walk.

My father always told me to walk when I was tired.

He said that no one ever fell asleep in the middle of a walk.

My father had died some years before in bed.

His words on sleep seemed especially important as a result.

Off I went into the night.

I walked up Bar Neck Road.

The night was quiet and I said so out loud.

When I had taken about thirty steps I turned and looked back at my house.

It was a riot of rectangles and triangles.

The upstairs windows looked like eyes.

My father had died in the right eye.

I turned away and went off down the road.

It was spring but it did not feel like spring.

I had been in Boston all winter long surrounded by trees but also by cold and I worried that I had lost the ability to relax into weather.

My reasons for going to Boston over the winter were stronger than my reasons for returning home in spring.

I had gone to forget a woman and I had returned because I thought I had forgotten her.

I had gone with another woman and I had returned when she was gone.

I made a right onto Albatross Road.

It was mild because it was spring but I shivered.

I still felt I was in winter and I said so out loud.

After the aquarium I turned onto Water Street and went up toward Luscombe Avenue.

The water was off to my right making the faintest noise as was the wind coming through the trees.

It was going right to left like a sentence being read in reverse.

The idea reminded me of the past and so I felt for my phone and called a woman.

She was not the same woman I had been seeing over the winter though they had the same name give or take.

One was named Gina and the other was named Regina.

Names were important in a situation like that.

I called.

This was the second thing I had to do.

She was home.

She was Regina.

I asked her if I could come over.

She said that would be nice.

She told me her husband was in Boston for the weekend.

I said that I hoped he was having a good weekend.

I vaguely remembered that he played in a band and I took a stab at the name.

One of those two things made her laugh.

She hung up the phone.

I went to her house up on School Street.

She opened the door before I knocked.

She was wearing a man's dress shirt and women's underwear.

She said she was psychic.

Then she said she wasn't psychic somewhat apologetically.

She said that she had seen me out the window.

I told her that I knew she wasn't psychic.

I told her that if she was really psychic she wouldn't have gotten married to her husband.

She told me not to mention him.

I said okay but reminded her that he was in Boston.

I told her that if she was really psychic she wouldn't have introduced me to Gina.

She told me not to mention her either.

I said okay but reminded her that Gina was in Maine.

I told her that everyone was so far away.

I told her that whoever was left should stick together.

I asked her if she wanted to take a walk.

She said that she was too tired.

She asked me if I wanted to come in.

I said that I would.

I went to the kitchen to open a bottle of wine.

Regina went to the couch and turned on the television.

The same cop show that I had been watching at home was still on.

There was a clock on a mantel over her.

It was an antique clock that was probably the most expensive thing in the house.

More than an hour had passed since the show started.

I expressed my confusion.

She said it was a two-hour season finale.

I didn't say anything.

She said she loved the show more than life itself.

I didn't say anything.

Once I had told her the same thing about herself.

At that time we were younger.

Back then she had a habit of wearing men's underwear and no shirt.

We had watched many television shows and almost always ended up in the same pleased position.

I had pledged my love and she had responded with an identical pledge.

We had decided that she would do away with her husband and come to me.

In my mind I saw it all play out and in my mind it was glorious.

My love for her was a blinding light and admitting that to myself did not feel melodramatic in the least.

Shortly after that my love for her had turned into something else.

I was not sure what it had turned into exactly.

It had turned into something darker and more solid.

It had started to darken when she told me that she was not sure that she could leave her husband and had solidified when one evening she introduced me to Gina.

She had told me that the two of us would get along nicely.

We did not.

I was still thinking constantly of Regina.

I did not know how I would get through the winter without her.

I got through it with Gina in Boston and mostly in bed.

From the outside it might have looked a little bit like love.

When she left to go back to Maine I felt nothing.

I did not even have a twinge of sadness seeing her go.

I returned to Woods Hole in the spring and my heart started racing.

Regina and I sat and watched the show.

The younger detective was certain he knew where the killer was hiding.

The older detective had his head buried in a file.

The female sergeant kissed the younger detective in a stairwell.

The older detective drank too much and looked at himself reproachfully in the mirror.

The killer got a job mopping floors in the police station.

The female sergeant had a dream that the younger detective shot and killed the older detective.

I poured us more wine and moved closer to her on the couch.

I was no longer tired.

I told her that I was tired earlier but had been revived by the walk.

I told her that I had taken the walk when I had remembered my father's advice.

She had known my father and at the mention of him she moved closer to me.

The outside of her thigh had a noticeable pulse that I always said was her leg's heartbeat.

She always told me that if it was pulsing that much on the outside of her leg I should feel the inside.

I did for a moment during the commercial.

That was the third thing I had to do.

When the show came back on she asked me what I thought would happen.

I said that I thought that the female sergeant's dream would come true.

She said no.

I was hoping she would say that she was not asking about the show.

I was hoping she would say that she was asking me what would happen with us.

I told her that.

She said no.

She said that the female sergeant had dreams every episode and they never came true.

She said they were supposed to be read as clues for future cases but that they had nothing to do with this episode's case.

I asked if the female detective was psychic.

She said that's what she meant by saying that her dreams were clues to future cases.

She told me to be quiet so we could watch the show.

A baby I did not recognize was rescued by a woman I did not recognize.

A man I did not recognize beat another man I did not recognize with a tire iron.

This elicited a gasp from Regina.

She said that the man might die.

I said that was too bad but that I would feel worse if I knew who he was.

A boy on a bicycle rode across the screen ringing his bicycle bell excitedly.

She asked me if it was that time already.

I told her I didn't know what she meant.

She explained that ten minutes before the end of every show there was some kind of scene like this.

Once it was a tugboat blowing its foghorn.

Once it was a dog leaping right at the camera.

She told me that the last ten minutes were always a doozy and this was a way of reminding audiences to stop getting snacks or going to the bathroom or talking.

I said that was interesting.

Or talking she said.

The older detective died of a heart attack.

The younger detective came upon the killer as he strangled a woman with a scarf.

The younger detective shot and killed the killer.

The female sergeant wept at the older detective's funeral as she held the hand of the younger detective.

The killer's funeral was not shown.

The show ended.

I did not like it any more than I had at the beginning.

I turned to tell her that I didn't see the appeal.

She was crying.

That prevented me from saying anything critical about the show.

I told her that my father had always told me that when I saw a woman crying I should do something about it.

She said she always liked my father.

She said that she was crying because she couldn't see me anymore.

She said she thought this was the last time.

She was standing right beside the antique clock.

Her words on time seemed especially important as a result.

She unbuttoned her men's dress shirt and pulled my hand inside it.

The touch of her skin created both pleasure and pain for me.

I withdrew my hand from both.

She said that she didn't know how she would get through the summer without it.

I agreed that it was a great show and much better than I had expected.

She took me to the bedroom.

She took off the shirt and the underwear.

She was not talking about the show anymore but she was still crying.

She told me that she thought something big was about to happen.

She said that if she had a bicycle bell she would ring it.

I told her that maybe she was psychic after all.

She pulled my hand toward her.

I withdrew my hand again.

This time there was more pain in it for me than pleasure.

I walked around the room.

I was so alert I thought I would never sleep again.

I found the shirt she had removed and wrapped one sleeve around each of my fists and placed the span of the shirt across her neck.

At first she was amused because she thought that I was making fun of the show.

Then she was excited because she thought that I was not.

Then she was terrified because she knew that I was not.

She tried to say my name and then her husband's name

and managed to say both in a sense which meant that she was saying neither.

She said my father's name which I did not understand.

She said no.

Her right eye went blind and the left eye soon followed.

I lowered her onto the bed.

That was the fourth thing I had to do.

I took the shirt and went back through the living room collecting the wine bottle which was the only other thing I had touched with my bare fingers.

I went out onto the road.

The night felt warmer and I said so out loud.

After twenty steps or so I turned and looked back at Regina's house.

The television was still on and its blue light flickered through the windows.

I turned back around and found a trash can and stuffed the bottle inside of it.

I found another trash can a half-block later and stuffed the shirt into it.

I went back up School Street just as I had come with nothing in my hands.

I drifted right and wondered what the sea and wind would sound like coming from my left.

I wondered if it would sound like a sentence being read forward.

Two policemen in a car passed by and gave a small wave and I gave an even smaller one.

I was minding my own business.

WHEN DEATH SHINES BRIGHT

BY DAVE ZELTSERMAN

Sandwich

Michael Yarrow drove to the quaint little sandwich shop in the quaint little downtown section of Sandwich and found that they had closed at five o'clock and he was fifty-five minutes too late. He stood for a moment trying to decide what to do. He hadn't eaten since that morning when he had finished the second half of the BLT that he'd brought back to his room the day before. It was December and these quaint little shops must close early in the off-season because the few other bakeries and cafés he had passed were also dark inside. He could go to the Daniel Webster Inn and eat in their tavern or spend twenty minutes and drive to Hyannis where he'd have no problem finding fast-food restaurants. There was also a chain donut shop and a chain convenience market a little past downtown. Michael Yarrow decided he didn't want to sit down among other people and he didn't feel like he had the energy to drive twenty minutes to Hyannis. He was also trying to limit the number of places he might be seen. The inn where he rented a room, the sandwich shop where he bought his food, and the liquor store where he bought beer. He decided he wasn't that hungry after all, and that he could pick up a couple strips of beef jerky and a bag of potato chips when he bought his beer, and that would be enough.

Michael got in his car to drive the three blocks to the liquor store, which would also take him out of this postage stamp–sized downtown. The buildings were either restored

Victorians or old Federal-style houses covered with weather-beaten shingles. A two-hundred-year-old church had been converted to a restaurant that was closed, and an even older church had been converted to shops. This was a town of money. Quiet, well kept up. But the first day Michael showed up, he had seen a couple of tiny cracks in the town's veneer. A sign advertising psychic readings. Another advertising *Gold Bought Here*. Only slight, tiny cracks, but still, it made Michael feel better.

Up until three days ago when he had come down from Somerville, Michael had never been to Sandwich or Cape Cod. He told Cheryl he was going to Atlantic City for a week to decompress after his first semester at medical school, but instead he drove here. Cheryl was his fiancée, had been for three years now. A blond, attractive girl with clear blue eyes and a nice shape, although maybe ten pounds too heavy. She would love this town. Even though there were only a couple dozen shops, she'd love each one of them, with their shelves of antique dollhouses and rocking horses and teddy bears. She'd love the glass museum, and even in this frigidly cold December weather, she'd probably love the boardwalk and the beach. There wasn't a chance that Michael would ever take her to Sandwich now.

The reason he was here was because of Fred Schwartz, one of his classmates at medical school. Schwartz and one of their other classmates, Joan Harris, would occasionally talk about Cape Cod, and Michael would eavesdrop on their conversations. Schwartz would always talk up Sandwich; about how quiet and peaceful it was, and how cheap this certain inn was during the off-season. Harris would always counter with Hyannis, about how much she enjoyed the bars and the rowdier atmosphere there. Hyannis sounded seedier to Michael, which was more to his liking, but when he decided to drive to the

Cape, he thought he'd be better off in a quieter area. He knew there was a state forest nearby, as well as a scenic beach, and he had images of himself bundling up in the cold and taking long walks by himself in both the forest and along the beach so he could soak up the solitude they'd provide. The first day he was here, he drove out to where the boardwalk was, which looked like a good half-mile over marshlands. Most of the boards had inscriptions carved in them, quite a few with little hearts, and he walked over about a hundred of these before he decided he'd had enough, and returned to his car without bothering to see the beach. He hadn't been back since then, nor had he bothered driving to the state forest, and instead spent most of his time in his room.

When Michael approached the liquor store he saw a scene that didn't fit with this quaint little town. Standing in the shadows was a feral-looking man in his late twenties wearing a hooded sweatshirt. He was thin and unkempt, with scruffy facial hair and long greasy locks hanging out from under his hood. Michael couldn't see the man's neck because of his sweatshirt and the darkness, but he guessed it was covered with tattoos. There was a wild, hyped-up look in the man's eyes, as if he was anxiously waiting for something. Seconds later the door to the liquor store opened and the girl who worked in the sandwich shop walked out carrying a package. She had taken maybe four steps when this man moved toward her. There was ill intent is his manner, and when the girl noticed him she froze, too startled to scream, not that it would've done her any good. Michael reacted without thinking, blasting his horn and then hitting the gas so he could accelerate forward and bring his car to a stop between the girl and the feral-looking man. The guy gave Michael a hard, angry, sullen looking before stepping back and disappearing into the shadows. Michael pressed the button to lower his passenger-side window.

"I hope I didn't scare you," he said, "but that didn't look good."

Her color had paled and she was visibly shaken. "Oh God," she said. "That was so bizarre. I think he was going to attack me."

"Do you know him?"

She shook her head.

Michael peered into the darkness where the feral sweat-shirted man had disappeared. "I think he's gone, but I don't want to take any chances. Can I drive you somewhere? Make sure you get home safely?"

"My car is three blocks away," she said.

"At the sandwich shop."

She squinted at him. As recognition hit, her lips pulled into a slight smile. "I thought you looked familiar. You've been coming to the shop the last couple of days. Sunday was turkey with havarti, yesterday was a BLT."

"That's right."

She looked around quickly and shivered. "He might still be out there," she said. "Sure, I'd like a ride."

She got into the passenger seat, and Michael gave her a thin smile as he backed into the street. She was an attractive girl. Not really a girl, more like twenty-three, only a few years younger than him. Her long red hair was pulled into a pony-tail. That and her slight build and thick glasses made her seem like a teenager, but she was still very pretty.

"I wouldn't think street muggings would happen in a place like Sandwich," Michael said.

Consternation momentarily ruined her brow. "This is a safe town. I've lived here all my life and never heard of any-thing like that happening here." Her voice trailed off into a soft murmur as she added, "It doesn't make sense, especially with the police station just down the road. Maybe he was only planning to panhandle money from me."

Michael shrugged. He didn't bother stating the obvious. As he drove he felt her again squinting at him.

"Why didn't you come to the shop today?" she asked. "Did you find a better place to eat?"

He shook his head. "Nope. I tried coming to the shop, but I came too late and you'd already closed up for the night. So I was going to the liquor store to pick up some beef jerky. And you know what happened next."

He pulled up in front of the shop where she worked, which had the appropriately quaint name The Sandwich Sandwich Shoppe. She hesitated for a moment before telling him that she would open up the shop for him and make him something to eat. "It's the least I can do for saving me," she said.

Michael didn't argue. He was hungry, and he liked the idea of spending some time with her. After leaving his car, she stopped and held out her hand. It was a small, delicate hand and it was cold to the touch because of the weather, but it still felt nice when Michael took hold of it.

"My name's Rachel," she said.

"Matt," he lied.

Once they were inside the shop, he told her he'd have a ham and cheese on a baguette, and she went about making him one, adding potato salad to the plate and also giving him a velvet chocolate cupcake, which she told him was their specialty. She also made him a roast beef and cheddar on a sourdough roll to take back with him to the inn. While he ate, she told him about life in Sandwich. After he was done, he offered to pay for his food but she told him it was on the house. "It's the least I can do for you coming to my rescue," she added, her eyes half-lidded and glistening.

He knew she wanted to spend more time with him, but he made an excuse for why he needed to call it a night, and he walked with her to her car to make sure she got to it okay. After that he went back to his car and drove again to the liquor store. This time he was able to buy a six-pack of Sam Adams lager without incident.

The inn where Michael was staying was less than a mile from downtown. The main house was an old restored Victorian, which had the nicer and more expensive rooms, but there was also, in the back, a row of connected single-room cottages. Michael had one of these cottage rooms, and it was pretty much generic—a queen-sized bed, a dresser, a chair, and a TV set, with a small attached bathroom that could barely fit a sink, toilet, and shower stall. While the rooms in the main house would be charming and more luxurious, the cottage had what he needed—it was cheap at thirty-nine dollars a day, which he paid with cash, and more importantly, it had its own entrance so there was less chance he'd be seen by other people every time he went in and out, which wasn't often.

Michael had a beer while he sat in the single chair in the room and fantasized about what it would've been like if he had brought Rachel back. Most women found him attractive, except for those times when he wasn't watching and something off would show in his eyes and his mouth would twist into something cruel. But usually he could keep that side of himself from other people. Cheryl had caught glimpses of him like that, but for whatever reason had chosen to ignore it.

Michael tried to imagine what Rachel would look like naked and what he would do to her body, but he was starting to feel too unsettled to hold that image in his mind. An anxiousness had been working in his stomach for days now and he was finding it harder to withstand. He hadn't called Cheryl since supposedly leaving for Atlantic City three days ago, and as much as he dreaded calling her now he didn't feel like he could put it off any longer. On his way to Cape Cod, he had stopped in Boston for a disposable cell phone. He used this to call Cheryl. When she answered, he apologized for not calling her earlier. "School put my head in a weird place. I needed some time alone to decompress and become human again," he told her.

"Okay," she said.

Her voice sounded so unnaturally brittle that it alarmed him. It was possible she was just sounding hurt because he didn't take her with him on his supposed trip to Atlantic City, or because he hadn't called her in three days, but it was also possible it was something else entirely. He felt his chest tightening as he waited for her to give him a clue which it was. When she didn't, he told her he missed her.

"How about I come down then and keep you company?" she asked with that same painful brittleness.

"It wouldn't be worth it," he told her. "I'll be home in a couple of days."

There was another long hesitation, which he could barely stand. Was Cheryl sincere or was there something going on? A numbness filled his head as he tried to figure it out.

"How come caller ID is showing your cell phone as unavailable?" she asked.

"I lost my phone and bought a disposable one," he lied. He still had his cell, and if everything worked out, he would tell her later how he found it in his car when he was driving home.

Her voice sounded normal again as she told him how she had tried calling him and was getting upset that he hadn't returned any of her calls. So that was it. He couldn't afford to keep his cell phone on since he knew he could be traced by it, so he didn't know that she had tried calling him. He should've guessed that was the case. So the police hadn't called her yet. He felt some relief realizing this, but only some. Still, he couldn't help asking whether anyone was looking for him.

"Why would anyone be looking for you?"

"I don't know. Maybe one of my professors or classmates."

"No one has called for you."

He told her he was hungry and was going to head down to the casino's buffet for dinner, but that he missed her and was looking forward to seeing her soon, and she told him the same. After disconnecting the call, he had another beer and found himself absently rubbing his right wrist. He rolled up his shirt-sleeve and saw that the scratches along his wrist were still red and ugly. Not nearly as bad as they had looked three days ago, but still pretty bad. He kept a tube of hydrocortisone cream near the chair, and he squeezed some out to rub on the scratch wounds. Hopefully in a few days they'd be gone.

The scratches were part of the reason he had taken off to the Cape without Cheryl. He couldn't afford to let anyone see them, especially not her. But the trip had also been to get some breathing room, so that no one would know where he was in case the police were looking for him. If the story broke that they were after him, he wanted a chance to run. He wasn't sure yet where he'd run, but he at least wanted that chance. He couldn't imagine letting the police arrest him.

Michael opened another beer and drank it slowly as he thought about the woman he had killed. She'd been a dancer in a strip club in East Boston. Five foot one, ninety pounds, she'd been a dark-haired beauty with smoldering eyes that still remained remote and distant. It was clear why the patrons in the strip club would stare at her. With her near perfect body and face and long flowing black hair, she was a creature of pure sexual fantasy, and she received by far the most tips of any of the dancers. This was why Michael had picked her, although he also liked that with her diminutive size she'd be more easily intimidated by him and less likely to put up a fight.

Last Saturday after the club had closed, he had followed

her, just as he had done two other times before. As she was cutting through a darkened alleyway from her car to the front door of her building, he was waiting with a knife to demand her money.

She should've just given it to him. When he'd robbed another strip club dancer four months earlier in Connecticut, she'd handed over her money and Michael had left her tied up but otherwise unhurt. The same would've happened Saturday, but this petite dark-haired beauty had tried to fight him, digging her claws into his wrist as she struggled for the knife. He'd reacted then without thinking, just flashing the knife out and somehow cutting her jugular. She'd stumbled backward onto the cement pathway, her life bleeding out very fast.

Michael panicked then. He hadn't expected to kill her. All he'd wanted was her money. He hadn't known if anyone had seen him or his car. After trying to brush any possible DNA evidence from under her fingernails, he'd taken her money and fled. It was only later that he'd realized she had bled over his coat, so he took it off and stashed it in the trunk of his car. He'd spent the rest of the night huddled in his car so Cheryl wouldn't see him. Early the next morning, he'd surprised her with his impromptu trip to Atlantic City. She'd been groggy from sleep, and he explained away the night before by saying he had gotten too drunk to drive home after an end-of-semester party and had slept on a classmate's sofa. This was an outrageous lie since he never spent any time socializing with any of his classmates. He still had his bloody coat stashed in the trunk, and planned to burn and bury it in the state forest before he left Sandwich.

One of the niceties that the inn provided was a complimentary copy of the *Boston Globe* each morning. When he'd killed her, Michael had only known the dancer's stripper name, which was Brandi, but her murder was a big story in the paper, and he learned her real name then, and that she was a single mother to a three-year-old daughter and was going to community college to be an accountant. From what he could tell from the newspaper stories, the police had no leads, but they were following up on inquiries. Each evening he watched the local news, but they had nothing about the story then.

So now he was a murderer, holed up in a motel room as he waited to know whether the police had anything, all for twelve hundred dollars that he had planned to use for a gambling excursion, just like he did with the money he stole from that other dancer.

He tried not to think of any of this. Instead he finished off his six-pack, then turned on the TV and sat quietly as it droned over any thoughts buzzing in his mind.

The *Globe* the next morning had nothing new about the murder. This left Michael more unsettled than before. It would almost be a relief if the police were onto him. At least then his next step would be clear. This waiting around was killing him.

He thought it would be good to get some fresh air, and maybe this time make it all the way down the boardwalk to the beach, but as he started to push himself out of his chair, he felt too listless for that, as if he didn't have the energy to move. Instead, he stayed holed up for another day. Around noon, he ate the roast beef sandwich Rachel had made him the night before, and then he just stared into space until six o'clock when he turned on the news. The top story was about breaking developments in the case of the dancer brutally murdered in East Boston four days before. Michael felt his insides freeze as he prepared to see his picture come up over the TV screen, but instead the police spokesman talked about how a former boyfriend had been arrested for the crime. When the camera showed a photo of this former boyfriend, Michael broke out laughing. The man was dark and swarthy, and had no resemblance whatsoever to Michael, which meant there were no witnesses. If he had been successful in removing any DNA evidence, he was in the clear.

He let out a loud exhalation. For the first time in days, he felt himself relax and the knots in his shoulder blades ease up. He still had to dispose of his bloodstained coat, and to be safe he should wait until his scratches were fully healed before heading home, but they were already much better. He had murdered a woman, but he would be a surgeon someday and would have the opportunity to save more than enough lives to make up for this.

He turned off the TV set and thought about what he had been through. He was honest with himself for the first time in weeks. He knew why that girl had fought him. He could feel the subtle shift in his features, and knew she had seen her death shining brightly in his eyes, even if it was only for a flash. That was why she had fought him, because she was fighting for her life, but she didn't have a chance. At a conscious level he had only been planning to rob her, but on another level he had been planning more. The thrill he had gotten from robbing the strip club dancer in Connecticut hadn't been enough. He didn't realize that at the time, only now.

He thought about Rachel. During the day he had been fantasizing about her. It was too early to play out his fantasies now, he'd have to wait a few months, and he'd have to learn how to steal a car so he could drive back here anonymously, but once he did, it would be easy enough. He would pull up to her sandwich shop a little after closing time and lure her into the stolen car. She was clearly attracted enough to him where it wouldn't be hard to do that, and he'd drive her someplace where no one would be able to hear her scream. He felt himself getting excited, and forced himself to take a deep breath and try to relax since it would be months before he'd be able to do this and see the fear shining brightly in her eyes as she saw her death shining just as brightly in his own.

It was twenty past six. Michael didn't feel like being with other people but he did feel like drinking, so he left his room to head out to the liquor store. Like every other day around this hour it was bitterly cold, with an almost impenetrable darkness as clouds hid the moon and stars. When he got to the liquor store, he rushed inside to escape the cold. He was ten feet into the store before he realized something was wrong. The feral-looking guy from the day before was standing in front of him pointing a gun at the clerk, his eyes every bit as hyped up and twitchy as they had been before. At first he turned to Michael with a blank hostility, but as recognition hit him, an all too familiar look flashed in his eyes.

Michael wanted to run, but before he could move, he felt a bullet slam into his skull. In that flash before the gunshot, he had seen his death shining in this other man's eyes, and before the darkness enveloped him, Michael knew what this feral-looking man was feeling. An overwhelming Godlike power over him. For the brief last moment that he was still alive he envied this man.

TWENTY-EIGHT SCENES FOR NEGLECTED GUESTS

BY JEDEDIAH BERRY

Yarmouth

For Emily

1.

In the illustration of the crime scene, the full moon is high and small over the sea, shining through a halo of cloud. The dark water reflects a thin, crooked finger of light. In the foreground, the beach is littered with black stones, bits of shell, seaweed, sea glass.

The body lies facedown in the sand, wedged between two large, thumb-shaped rocks. The hair is long and stringy; it obscures the face and spreads across the ground like the head of a mop. One slender arm is draped over a rock, and the other is hidden by the fabric covering most of the body. A mourning dress? A costume? It clings to the flesh of the corpse, all ragged black folds. The bare feet stick out from beneath it, toes angled toward the water. They appear carefully poised, like the feet of a dancer.

And then there's the dog. Black and round, a mutt with stubby legs and floppy ears, it's not the kind of dog you'd expect to discover a corpse, at least not in any official capacity. The dog holds itself rigid, something like pride in its stance, snout aimed at the body.

Not just at the body, but at the exposed right forearm which, upon closer inspection, reveals a tattoo along the length of its inner side. The flowing, ornamental script is impossible to decipher at this angle. A clue? Yes, this could be a clue.

The dog's paw prints are visible in the sand. Hours ago, there may have been other prints to read—the victim's, the killer's—but if they were here, the sea has washed them away.

2.

The Untoward Specter, cloaked all in black crepe, sits weeping in the gazebo. "Is it time for a game of pies?" it asks.

The Three Widows of North Varnish clutch their bosoms. "But we do not know how to play," they cry.

Lord Lumpish leans from the balcony and heaves a great sigh. "I do not permit games to be played upon the greensward," he says.

From a distance comes the squeak and shuffle of a handcar. The Three Widows of North Varnish put their hands over their ears, but the Untoward Specter looks up and stops weeping. It sways from side to side, as though mesmerized by the sound. "I should like very much to teach you how to play a game of pies," it says.

3.

I should like very much to knock that woman over the head, thinks Carl. He's playing the part of all three widows, a thin rustling dress on each hand and one draped over his face. But this woman Alex—loud, hysterical Alex from no-one-seems-to-know-where—is upstaging all three of him. And she the newcomer, her first show with the troupe, her first time onstage anywhere, as far as he knows. Correction: she's the kind of woman who has been onstage her whole life.

The widows aren't easy to operate. A lot of string-pulling to move their little arms, to make them titter and swoon. In his best elderly treble, Carl says, "That terrible sound! Is it the handcar of the Hands of the Orphans?"

But before the line is fully out of Carl's mouth, before he can even get Widow Number Three to point to the horizon, Alex calls from the gazebo, "I am certain the Hands of the Orphans will want to play a game of pies!"

Carl is about to throw the damned widows off his hands, but then he hears Ted cooing his approval from the front row. Ted, whose mess this whole thing is. Ted, who spends maybe five percent of his time in the real world.

"Everyone!" cries the Untoward Specter, louder than before. "Everyone must play or no one at all!"

Now Ted is clapping with quiet glee. *Yes,* thinks Carl, *right over the head, with something blunt and very heavy.*

4.

Aggie's hands hurt. Not from the hour spent pulling bent nails out of a broken panel of the set (gray sky, black clouds, a distant tower), but from the role she has landed without meaning to. Ted had stopped her on the first day of rehearsals, while she was carrying lumber into the theater. "Your hands," he'd said. "*Those* are the hands of the Hands of the Orphans."

His own fingers were decked with enormous iron rings, weird totems that clacked and gleamed when he gestured. The rings, and the beard, and the ratty tennis shoes: for a moment she mistook him for a crazy person who'd wandered into the theater. Then he showed her the puppets he'd made for the play he'd written, the play she was building sets for. Onto her hands he slipped a pair of black felt gloves. At the end of each finger was a grasping, desperate little child's hand.

At first Aggie thought they were terrible. All those sprouting pale nubs, like an animal they'd keep in a tank at the science aquarium. But now she feels, somehow, that the hands need her, and she can't go anywhere without them. On break from rehearsal, while the others go to a sandwich shop, she takes her bagged lunch to a bench by the shore and sets the Hands of the Orphans beside her.

"Do you think Carl likes me?" she asks the hands. She sips coffee from her thermos and nods. "Mmm, yes, he does have very nice eyes."

5.

Lord Lumpish stands with hands clasped behind his back, admiring the tapestries. The Untoward Specter appears at dusk. It glides down the hall, rustling as it swoons.

"I have a craving for sea air," the Untoward Specter says, "and the Hands of the Orphans have offered to arrange an excursion."

Lord Lumpish fiddles with his cuff links. "I fear that none of us are ready for a game of pies," he says.

6.

In his usual booth at Jack's Outback, Ted sits with his grilled cheese, bacon, and tomato on white bread, his fruit cup in a bowl. Because fruit cup in a cup just isn't enough fruit cup.

He's nervous about *Neglected Guests*. Something is lacking in the third act. The Three Widows of North Varnish have a secret he can't quite get at. He, who made them with his own two hands.

No, what's really bothering him is that he can't place what's bothering him. It makes him grumpy, having to worry about all these other people. And yet every summer, another script dashed off, more puppets, more rehearsals. *Actors!* They're the very opposite of cats, always wanting you to know what they think.

There's one last grape in his bowl. He tries to get it onto his fork, but the grape rolls and rolls, eluding him.

"Get you your check?" asks Ellie.

"No!" Ted says, much louder than he'd intended, and he and Ellie both are startled.

7.

Perry climbs onto the deck of the *Murasaki* and holds up a paper bag full of egg sandwiches. "Egg sandwiches!" he says. He made them himself.

The other guys working the restoration job set down their hammers and chisels and brushes. They shuffle over and take the wrapped packages from the bag, muttering thanks.

"I get to wear a beard in this play I'm in," Perry says. "I'm like some kind of king, you know? I have my own greensward."

The others pass around a bottle of ketchup.

"The guy who wrote it is crazy, just crazy. He's directing too. You know who he is. That poster, with all the kids and how they died? It's hilarious."

One of them says between mouthfuls, "Yeah, dead kids, funny," and the others chuckle.

"Everyone in the play is awesome and we all get along great," Perry says. "I mean, I don't like them better than I like you guys or anything."

They're all chewing, looking at their feet or at the water or at other boats.

"Though there is this one girl," he says.

This gets their attention for a moment, but Perry knows how that will go: the whistles, the ugly winks and uglier questions.

"Anyway," he says, "the show's this weekend. You should all come! Wait till you see the part about the pies."

For a moment the others think maybe he brought pies in addition to the sandwiches, but then they figure out that he's still talking about the play, and they shake their heads and wipe their mouths on their shirtsleeves and get back to work.

8.

Aggie, at home, has to take off the Hands of the Orphans so she can answer the phone. It's Jared. He sounds like he's trying to swallow something.

"I have bad news," Jared says. It's about Otto, the dog. Their dog, though he lives with Jared now.

Aggie tries to keep to the facts. "What does the vet say?"

"I have to bring him back on Tuesday. But it doesn't look good."

"What does that mean, *doesn't look good?*"

Jared's voice goes hard. "Look, I thought you might want to know. So you can make time to see him, if it comes to that."

"Comes to *what*, Jared?"

"I shouldn't have called," he says, and then there's another voice in the background—*Honey?* it says, or is Aggie imagining things?—and then the line goes dead.

9.

At the bar, Carl takes his beer onto the deck and finds Alex alone, staring out over the pond. He touches her shoulder and says, "Listen, I feel like things are all wrong between us. Maybe we can talk this out."

"Things are all wrong between us?"

"Come on."

She brings her face to within a few inches of his and says, "Take your hand off my shoulder, Carl."

He pulls away as though he's been burned. "It's Perry, isn't it?"

She doesn't answer, but he swears he can feel some kind of heat coming off her. And something else, like maybe she enjoys this.

"Poor, simple Perry," he says. "That your kind of guy?"

He grabs her shoulder again and moves to kiss her, but Alex hits him in the gut and knocks his beer off the railing. In the moment that he flails for it, she heads for the door. *Plop!* goes the mug into the water, and Alex is gone too.

10.

They take five, so Aggie brings her tools out to the truck. The sets are done, and she'll need her own things if she's going to finish those cabinets Ted wants for his place. She tosses the bag onto the floor of the cab, then climbs into the passenger seat and gets her cigarettes and lighter out of the glove box.

"Just one," she says to the Hands of the Orphans, which are nestled on her lap.

The window is still spotted with Otto's dried slobber, though it's been months since he's ridden in her truck. She keeps the window cracked while she smokes.

"The thing about Carl," she says, "is that we're both people who work with our hands."

11.

En route to the shore, Lord Lumpish operates the handcar while the Untoward Specter acts as lookout. The Three Widows of North Varnish sit at the back, knitting scarves for their cats.

"I am not certain that fewer than three terrible things will happen to us today," says the Untoward Specter.

"Are there any more cabbage sandwiches?" the widows want to know.

"If we must play a game of pies," says Lord Lumpish, "I would like to be the baker. But who will be the pies?"

"The Hands of the Orphans will be the pies!" announces the Untoward Specter. "But where have they gone?"

"Here they are," say the widows, who have accidentally knitted them into their scarves.

The Hands of the Orphans squirm in the yarn as the hand-car rolls into a tunnel.

12.

Rehearsal runs late, and Carl misses the last ferry back to the Vineyard. Aggie offers to put him up at her place.

"Nothing special, but it's cozy," she says, and there's something about the way she chooses these words. Like she herself is figuring out what she has to offer.

He follows her pickup out of town and onto a winding road off Route 2. The cottage looks like an Arts and Crafts throwback; she probably built the place herself. She leads him inside—front door isn't locked—and he stands in the kitchen while she goes through the house, turning on lights in every room. "Open a bottle?" she calls.

There's a little rack on the counter. None of the wines look good, but he settles on a Malbec that can't be terrible. He's rummaging through drawers, looking for a corkscrew, when he hears a man's voice on the answering machine in the next room. Then hears, after a minute, the sound of Aggie weeping.

He sets the bottle down and walks into what probably used to be a dining room but is now a woodworking studio. Tools everywhere, and buckets of stain, and on a table a set of finished cabinets.

"Hey," he says. "Hey, what happened?"

She's sitting on the floor by the phone, rubbing her eyes with her fists. "Wednesday's going to be my last day with Otto before he dies."

Those cabinets are beautiful. Maybe he ought to hire her sometime.

"God, I'm so sorry," he says, and kneels beside her. "Who's Otto?"

Then Aggie has her arms around him, and her mouth is against his, and she's moving her lips and nibbling.

He pushes her away. "I don't think—"

She appears to wither a little, but she doesn't start crying again. "You can take the bedroom," she says, nodding toward the hall. "We'll take the couch."

"We?"

She looks startled, and her hand goes defensively to her pocket. Sticking out from it are five pale little hands.

13.

Perry drives out to Truro, to pick up Alex before rehearsal. She's staying at her uncle's place for the summer. The house is on a dirt road off another dirt road, at the top of a hill overlooking a salt marsh.

When she answers the door, she isn't wearing pants.

"Wow, hi," Perry greets her.

"I'll be just a minute," she says.

He follows her inside and closes the door behind him. He tries not to look at her thighs, but she snaps the elastic of her blue underpants as she goes into the bedroom. There are sounds of drawers opening and closing. "Hey," she calls out to him, "if you were going to kill Carl, how would you do it?"

Alex is a year or two older than Perry, maybe twenty-eight, and he wants to be able to keep up with her. But he just laughs and can't think of what to say.

"Something sharp, maybe?" she says. "Right through the eye? Or something weird. Some kind of poisonous sea creature on his chair."

Perry says, "Hey, do you think Carl and Aggie—"

"Nope," she cuts him off. "No way."

There's some kind of altar set up on the kitchen table, looking out of place here. Perry bends down for a closer look:

candles, a glass skull full of clear liquid, round tarot cards, old photos, bits of fur, scraps of paper with names and phrases written on them, and something that looks like a narwhal tusk. He reaches out to touch it but Alex says, "Don't touch that."

She's standing right behind him, dressed in the black pants and shirt that will disappear beneath the Untoward Specter costume.

"Are you some kind of witch?" he asks.

"Yes."

He can't tell if she's serious.

"I'm working on a spell," she says. "That's the real reason I'm here. It'll make me forget everyone and everything I never want to think about again."

"Well, I hope you'll let me know if it works."

"Oh, you'll know," she says.

14.

"My husband died because he ate too much," says the first of the three Widows of North Varnish. "Too much poison, that is."

"And my husband died because he hit his head," says the second widow, "against the skillet I was holding."

"As for my husband," says the third widow, "he died of natural causes."

"Is that so?" asks the first widow.

"We were standing together on the edge of a very high cliff, just admiring nature, and then he fell right into it."

The three widows huddle close, giggling.

Ted leaps from his seat and onto the stage. "Stop! Stop!"

Carl lifts the skirt of the middle widow off his sweaty face. Final dress rehearsal, and he's never seen Ted looking so distressed.

"This isn't working," Ted says, rings clinking as he waves his hands. "We'll have to strike this scene."

"But—" Carl starts to say, his voice cracking because it's still half widow. He coughs. "But Ted, it's the funniest bit in the whole damn piece."

"It is an incontestable disaster. We'll have to go from the Devil Costume Mix-Up straight to the waltz of the Untoward Specter. Alexandra. Alexandra! Kiddo, can you manage this?"

The wrinkled black figure shuffles out from behind the set. "Yes," Alex says, fixing the folds of her costume. "Yes, sure, that's fine."

"Carl," Ted says, "do stay onstage, please. The specter can push the widows aside as it enters. That should get a laugh."

Carl blinks; the salt of his sweat is burning his eyes.

"Here," Alex says to him, "let me help you," and she pulls the skirt down over his face.

15.

Aggie loads the finished cabinets onto the bed of her pickup and drives to Ted's place in Yarmouth. The house is covered with vines on one side, and the other side is partially devoured by an overgrown rhododendron. She climbs the sunken porch steps and knocks on the door, which is sorely in need of paint.

There's some quiet shuffling within, and Aggie knows she's being scrutinized from one window or another. Then the door opens, and Ted's pale, bald, bearded face looms into view. His eyes are dark and unhappy—no trace there of the diligent whimsy she's come to know at the theater.

"Agatha, you're early," he says, and from the dimness beyond comes the quiet plunk of a cat landing on the floor.

"Wrapped up sooner than I thought."

He lets her in, and even tries to help her carry the cabinets, though she manages fine on her own. Inside the house, piled on tables and shelves, and scattered over the floor, is all the outrageous clutter of a thousand odd pursuits. Old glass bottles, blue telephone pole insulators, dolls, clothing irons, ancient-looking cheese graters, piles of CDs, skulls, stuffed animals. A shriveled thing she knows to be a real mummy's hand. Bowls of marbles. Stray amulets and rings. Marionettes, newspapers, books everywhere, and everywhere the cats, four or five or six of them, coming and going, dozing in high places. The couches and chairs are devastated by their attentions.

Once she sets to work mounting the cabinets in his studio, Ted appears cheerier. He makes tea and brings two cups upstairs, talks to her about the play while she works. His drafting table is here, and it's hard not to steal glances at the little book he's working on. One illustration depicts three willowy figures, a man and two women. One of the women has just knocked the other over the head with what looks like a doorknob. On another page, a man in a fur coat is about to be crushed by an enormous urn.

Ted sees her looking and says, "All those tiny murders we think about but never make happen. I don't know where I'd be without them."

The cabinets are ready. "What will you keep in here?" she asks.

"Oh, well, this and that." He stands and runs a hand over the door. "Spiffy!" he says.

On her way out, while they're saying goodnight, Aggie feels the urge to tell him about Otto, about Carl, about the fact that she's been sneaking the puppets home with her every night. She touches his arm, and a shocked look appears on his face, then quickly stows itself behind a strained smile.

Ted looks very tired again. "See you at the theater," he says.

16.

Carl has invited everyone out to his place on the Vineyard. In the morning, Aggie drives to Jared's house to pick up Otto. Jared starts to say something about how he'll be at the play, but she hurries off, telling him that she has to catch the ferry.

The entire cast and crew (except for Ted, who declined the invitation with an embarrassed fluttering of his hands) meet at the Steamship Authority. On board, Alex sits across the table from Aggie and says, "Do you know how long it's been since I've . . . you know?"

The Hands of the Orphans are hidden on Aggie's lap. She squeezes their fingers.

"Two and a half years!" says Alex.

Aggie doesn't know whether or not she's supposed to believe her.

"Do you believe me?" Alex asks.

"I'm not sure what we're talking about."

Alex takes a white marble from her pocket and sets it on the table. The marble rolls slowly one way, then the other. It goes right to the edge of the table and stops there. Aggie holds her breath, waiting for it to fall, but Alex grabs it just before it drops.

"What does your tattoo mean?" Aggie asks.

Alex keeps her arms extended, turning it over so the script is in the light. It runs from her wrist to the crook of her arm, all angles, swoops, and dots. "It's Tibetan for one of the four immeasurables," she says. "But I forget which."

17.

Around his property, among the trees and on the grassy slope down to the beach, Carl has erected dozens of wood and metal sculptures. Some have faces, some are just hands. "Derelict things," he calls them. "I make them in my spare time."

One has spinning windmill sails on top of its large, Buddha-like body. Perry reaches out to touch it.

"Don't touch that," Carl says.

He puts on an old jazz record. Everyone sits on blankets and opens picnic baskets. Otto scampers among them while they eat, begging bits of meat from their sandwiches. Then one of the stagehands leans back and bellows, "I wish I knew how to play a game of pies!"

"This is supposed to be a break," says Carl.

Alex stands up and bunches the front of her skirt into her hands, as though preparing to run. "I should like *very* much to teach you how to play."

Perry, stammering a bit, says, "Right here, upon the greensward?"

"Right here," Alex answers, staring straight at Carl. "Right here upon the greensward, and to hell with what old Lord Lumpish thinks."

18.

The baker is hard at work, and the kitchen is hot, hot! He's rolling out a fresh batch of dough when he hears a knocking at the door. Who could it be? A customer?

The baker goes to the door, opens it just a little, and peers outside. "Who's there?" he asks, though the baker can see who's there. It's the devil with the dirty face and hands.

"The devil with the dirty face and hands," says the devil.

"Go wash your dirty face and hands!" the baker says.

The devil sighs and goes to the well. He draws up a bucket of water, kneels over it, and washes his dirty face and hands. Then he returns to the baker's door and knocks again.

"Who's there?" the baker asks.

"The devil with the clean face and hands."

"Well, come right in!" the baker says.

Now the devil is feeling fine. He likes it here in the hot, hot kitchen. He can smell good things cooking. "Do you have any pies today?" asks the devil.

"Of course I have pies," the baker says. "Can't you hear them clapping in the oven?"

19.

They go for a walk on the beach together. Otto weaves among their legs, grabbing pieces of driftwood and barking at the ones he can't get his jaws around.

Alex picks up a stick and throws it for the dog to fetch. Watching him run, she says, "He doesn't look like he's dying."

"I know," says Aggie. "But Jared tells me he cries all night. It's some kind of cancer."

"You're doing the right thing, absolutely," says Carl.

"Because you're the death expert," says Alex.

"Ted's the death expert," says Carl.

"Death expert!" says Perry, and does a flying jump kick.

Aggie kneels as Otto comes back. He drops the stick at her feet, and she rubs his round head with both hands, flopping his ears. Then she sees that it isn't a stick he brought back. It's an old umbrella, just a few strips of fabric still clinging to its broken ribs.

20.

"Can't you hear them clapping in the oven?" the baker asks.

The oven door opens a little, and the Hands of the Orphans emerge. They all begin to clap, and the sound is like rain, or like radio static.

"I do hear them clapping!" the devil says. "Do you have any strawberry pie?"

The baker glances at the Hands of the Orphans, and the hands recoil. "I'm sorry," he says, "no strawberry today."

"What about peach?"

The Hands of the Orphans turn and turn.

"No," says the baker, "no peach."

The devil is getting impatient now. He taps one hoof against the floor. "How about cream pie?" he asks. "Surely you have some cream pie?"

"Cream pie," the baker says. "Well, let me see."

The Hands of the Orphans all are trembling.

21.

Aggie wakes to the sound of Otto whimpering next to her bed. She switches on the light and sees him lying on his side on the blue carpet, his open eyes rolled back into his head. His legs are twitching, as though from a dream of running.

She gets down next to him and strokes his head, whispers his name. Then she sees, next to him on the carpet, one of the Hands of the Orphans. The other is a few feet away, near the nightstand. She had left them both on a chair at the other end of the room.

She picks up the nearer puppet and finds it damp with slobber. The fabric is shredded, and the hands themselves have been chewed to pieces. Fragments of fingers and thumbs are scattered over the floor, and Aggie remembers, now, that she had heard a crunching sound in her sleep.

"Bad dog!" she screams at Otto. "Bad, bad dog!" and hits him in the ribs with her fists.

Otto is still whimpering, still moving his legs. Her blows turn to soft thumps, and then she stops hitting him and buries her face in his fur. She listens to Otto's heartbeat. "Just die if you need to," she says, but she hopes he can't hear her.

22.

Neglected Guests
A Worrisome Diversion by E___ G___
Thursday–Saturday, 8 p.m.

A dreary sight upon the shore has made a horror of their tour.

23.

Wearing her costume over her jeans, Alex takes the path down to the beach. No one knows she brought the Untoward Specter home with her. It seemed right for the occasion, so she had to have it. Her pockets are full of paper, and on each torn scrap is written the name of somebody or something she would like to forget.

With the waves lapping at her bare feet, she removes the scraps one at a time, reads aloud what's on them, and tosses them into the wind.

When she's finished, she walks for a while along the beach, then sits between two rocks shaped like big thumbs. There's supposed to be a full moon tonight, and that, she realizes, is the only thing she's sure about.

Alex shivers, takes a deep breath. "It worked," she says.

24.

Carl calls Perry and says, "Hey, you're giving Alex a ride to the big show tonight?"

"Sure am," Perry says.

"Listen, I'm going to be in P-town today—have to pick up some things for a piece I'm working on. So I'll just grab her on my way back."

"Oh, well—"

"So what's the address?" Carl asks.

"Maybe I should give her a call first," says Perry, and that's all Carl needs to hear to know that, *Yes, these two are definitely sleeping together.*

"In a hurry here, my man. Just give me the address, all right?"

Perry agrees, of course—would probably give you his own pants if you asked for them—and Carl heads out to Truro early.

It feels good to drive for more than ten minutes, and he takes Route 6 a little faster than he needs to.

He finds the place without much trouble, though it's secluded, at the end of a long dirt road. No answer at the door, so he wanders around the house. Would Perry have given him the wrong address? He peers through a window, sees nothing but modern furniture and a nice stereo system. But there's a path down the hill, and if Carl has his directions right, it must lead right to the beach.

There's a solid-looking walking stick in a bucket by the back porch. He takes that and heads for the trail.

25.

"What's this?" says Lord Lumpish, kneeling on the shore. Dozens of scraps of paper litter the beach. He takes one of them in his gloved hand.

"There's something written on it," say the widows, leaning close.

"*My father,*" Lord Lumpish reads aloud. "That's all it says."

The Hands of the Orphans gather more scraps and hold them up for Lord Lumpish to read.

"*The neighbor's son. The lake. The year I turned thirteen.*"

"Is it a story?" say the widows. "Someone's fortune?"

"*What happened in the kitchen,*" reads Lord Lumpish. "*All my lines. The way home.*"

"Well, that's enough of that," say the widows.

Just then a black dog comes running toward them along the strand. It leaps excitedly on its short legs, gesturing with its snout in the direction from which it came.

The widows are wringing their hands. "I do believe there's something it wants us to see," they say.

Only when they prepare to set out do they realize that the Untoward Specter has vanished.

26.

The devil must have pie. But the devil must guess what kind of pie before he can have it. Those are the rules.

"How about rutabaga?" the devil asks.

"Sorry," says the baker. "There is no rutabaga pie."

"Melancholy meringue? Please tell me you have some of that."

"No, nothing in the way of melancholy meringue."

"Umbrella pie?" the devil asks, leaning close. "You do have umbrella pie, don't you?"

"Well," says the baker, "let's take a look."

27.

Just an hour before curtain, and the production is in complete disarray. Ted stalks back and forth behind the stage, trying to direct the men in charge of the lighting. It's as though none of them have even seen a lightbulb before.

Carl jogs up to him, out of breath.

"There you are," Ted says. "Why aren't you in costume?"

"Nobody can find Alex," Carl answers. "I went out to her place myself; no sign of her. I think she might have packed up and gone."

"Maybe she's with—"

But there's Perry, looking shaken. "I drove up there too," he says. "When I didn't hear from her."

The two men stare at one another. Ted thinks: *I should have stayed home, I should have just stayed home.* He walks slowly to the front of the stage and collapses on the chaise lounge. The cast and crew gather around him. "Where is Alexandra from?" he asks, but no one says anything. "Doesn't anybody know where she's from?" His hands are moving, his rings clacking. "This is the worst thing that has ever happened. I'll have to play the

Untoward Specter myself. But I can't perform the waltz!"

"We'll put the bit about the widows' dead husbands back in," says Carl. "That'll patch it up."

Perry looks lost, is walking in circles under the uneven lights, and then the theater door bursts open. Aggie comes down the aisle, face pale, eyes red, hair a mess. She's carrying something bundled in her hands.

Ted sits up. "What is it?" he says. "What's happened?"

Aggie holds out the bundle. It's a mass of torn fabric and broken fingers and thumbs. It shakes because Aggie is shaking. She holds it up, as though to make an offering, and several digits fall to the floor.

28.

A black dog walks alone on the beach. He has been walking a long time. Sometimes he wanders close to the water, fleeing when a wave advances upon him, barking as the wave retreats. When the tide goes out, the dog discovers things that feel good to carry and chew. A tattered black glove. The hooked wooden handle of an umbrella. A fragment of some sea animal's tusk.

Often the dog catches on the air the scent of people, a few of them at least, just upwind. He runs in their direction but doesn't catch them. They must be very quick.

But that's fine, because there's plenty here to keep a dog busy: scurrying creatures to chase, birds that pop into the air when you run at them, things to find and bury in the sand. And the dog is possessed by the sense, urgent and profound and brimming with the promise of love and praise, that soon, very soon now, he will discover something important. That he has only to wait until the sun goes down before a great mystery is solved.

And then maybe someone will give him something to eat.

ABOUT THE CONTRIBUTORS

Lucy Hamblin

JEDEDIAH BERRY'S first novel, *The Manual of Detection* (The Penguin Press, 2009), was awarded the Hammett Prize from the International Association of Crime Writers, as well as the Crawford Award from the International Association for the Fantastic in the Arts. His stories have appeared in journals and anthologies including *Conjunctions, Chicago Review, Best American Fantasy,* and *Best New American Voices.* Invaluable assistance on the story appearing in this book was provided by Marty Thomas.

James Goodwin

DANA CAMERON'S first Anna Hoyt story, "Femme Sole" (in *Boston Noir*) was nominated for the Edgar, Anthony, Agatha, and Macavity awards. Her story here, set in the 1740s, was inspired by research at Great Island and the village of Wellfleet, which was part of Eastham until 1763. Whether writing noir, historical fiction, urban fantasy, or traditional mystery, Cameron's crime novels and short fiction draws on her expertise in New England archaeology. She lives in Beverly, Massachusetts.

Melisa Heltzel

ELYSSA EAST is the author of the *Boston Globe* best seller, *Dogtown: Death and Enchantment in a New England Ghost Town.* A *New York Times* Editors' Choice selection, *Dogtown* won the 2010 L.L.Winship/PEN New England Award for best work of nonfiction and was named a "Must-Read Book" by the Massachusetts Book Awards. Her essays and reviews have been published in the *New York Times, Philadelphia Enquirer, Dallas Morning News, Kansas City Star,* and other publications nationwide.

Allegra Greenland

SETH GREENLAND is a novelist and playwright. His novels include *Shining City, The Bones,* and the forthcoming *The Angry Buddhist.* His first play, *Jungle Rot,* was the recipient of the Kennedy Center/American Express Fund for New American Plays Award and the American Theatre Critics Association Award. His other produced plays include *Jerusalem, Red Memories,* and *Girls in Movies.* He first visited Cape Cod as a five-year-old.

Gail Gbezzi

BEN GREENMAN is an editor at the *New Yorker* and the author of several acclaimed books of fiction, including *Superbad, Please Step Back,* and *What He's Poised to Do.* His most recent book is *Celebrity Chekhov.* He lives in Brooklyn.

WILLIAM HASTINGS is a graduate student in the Solstice low-residency creative writing MFA program of Pine Manor College. While living on the Cape he worked as a golf course maintenance man, a special needs teacher, a middle and high school English teacher, and as a full-time waiter and prep cook. Besides Cape Cod, he has also lived in upstate New York, Colorado, Pennsylvania, the island of St. John, Denmark, Mexico, and Kuwait.

William Hastings

KAYLIE JONES is the author of the acclaimed memoir *Lies My Mother Never Told Me* and the novels *A Soldier's Daughter Never Cries* (which was released as a Merchant Ivory Film), *Celeste Ascending*, and *Speak Now*. She has contributed to the *Los Angeles Times*, the *New York Times*, the *Paris Review*, the *Washington Post*, and others. Jones teaches at SUNY-Stony Brook's Southampton College MFA Program in Writing, and in the low-residency MFA Program in Professional Writing at Wilkes University.

William Prystauk

FRED G. LEEBRON is the program director of the MFA in creative writing at Queens University of Charlotte and a Professor of English at Gettysburg College. His novels have been published by Knopf, Doubleday, and Harcourt, and his stories appear frequently in magazines such as *Tin House, TriQuarterly, The Threepenny Review*, and elsewhere, and have been selected for both Pushcart and O.Henry prize anthologies.

James Hale

ADAM MANSBACH'S novels include *The End of the Jews*, winner of the California Book Award, and the best-selling *Angry Black White Boy*. The 2010–11 New Voices Professor of Fiction at Rutgers University, his forthcoming projects include a graphic novel, *Nature of the Beast*, and a children's book, *Go the Fuck to Sleep*.

Victoria Häggblom

LIZZIE SKURNICK is the author of *Shelf Discovery*, a memoir of teen reading. She writes on books and culture for the *New York Times*, the Daily Beast, Politics Daily, the *Los Angeles Times, Bookforum*, and many other publications. A former vice-president of the board of the National Book Critics Circle, she is also the author of a book of poetry, *Check-In*. She lives in Jersey City.

Casey Greenfield

PAUL TREMBLAY is the author of the weird-boiled novels *The Little Sleep* and *No Sleep Till Wonderland*, and the short story collection *In the Mean Time*. His short fiction has appeared in *Weird Tales* and *Real Unreal: Best American Fantasy, Volume 3*. He has coedited a number of anthologies and can beat any crime writer in a game of one-on-one basketball. He still has no uvula and lives somewhere south of Boston with his wife and two kids.

DAVID L. ULIN is book critic, and former book editor, of the *Los Angeles Times*. He is the author of *The Lost Art of Reading: Why Books Matter in a Distracted Time* and *The Myth of Solid Ground: Earthquakes, Prediction, and the Fault Line Between Reason and Faith*. His work has appeared in the *Atlantic Monthly*, the *Nation*, the *New York Times Book Review*, *Bookforum*, *Columbia Journalism Review*, and on NPR's *All Things Considered*. He has spent summers on Cape Cod for forty years.

DAVE ZELTSERMAN lives in the Boston area, and is the author of the "man out of prison" crime trilogy: *Small Crimes*, *Pariah*, and *Killer*. *Small Crimes* and *Pariah* were both picked by the *Washington Post* as best books of the year. His recent *The Caretaker of Lorne Field* was shortlisted by the ALA for Best Horror Novel of 2010. His latest, *Outsourced*, has been optioned by Impact Pictures and Constantin Film and is currently under development.

F. Brett Cox

Noab Ulin

Judy Zeltserman